THE FORGE OF THE COVENANT

COVENANT

Raven Son: Book Four

NICHOLAS KOTAR

WAYSTONE
PRESS

THE FORGE OF THE COVENANT

(Raven Son: Book Four)

Copyright © Nicholas Kotar 2019

Cover Design by Books Covered Ltd.

Published by Waystone Press 2019

ISBN: 9780998847986

❀ Created with Vellum

For Daniel

CHAPTER 1

THE DEAD SIRIN

L ebía didn't realize how tense she was until the whispering intimacy of the beech grove enveloped her. Her shoulders melted like hot wax, and the pleasure of the release continued all the way to her toes. She almost sighed aloud, but stopped herself in time. Appearances, she reminded herself, even when picking mushrooms.

A Dar's wife must always preserve appearances. If she didn't, her daughters certainly would remind her of it.

"Mama, what about this one?" asked Zabían, her five-year-old son, his voice rising to the last syllable as though he wasn't asking a question, but demanding why there was so much injustice in the world. Everything he said had that intense inflection. He showed her a lovely brown mushroom with a cap like a perfect cloud, white gills underneath, not a spot marring their perfection. Their *deadly* perfection, that is.

"You see that?" she showed him the top of the cap. "Honey mushrooms have brown spots there, darker than the rest of the cap. That's a rotter, that is."

"And you forgot to look for the black ring," added Adelaida, her eldest, her face mostly hidden behind a stiff red-gold head-scarf. She still managed to glower at Zabían. "Honey mushrooms have a black ring under the cap, remember?" What she didn't say aloud, but what seemed to echo through the sun-dappled grove anyway, was something like, *how many times have I told you that? Five thousand?*

Lebía smiled. She didn't fault Adelaida for her seriousness. She *was* the eldest and most burdened with the care of the other children. To her surprise, Lebía felt a twinge of guilt. She really shouldn't spoil Zabían so much. Poor Adelaida always had the hardest of it, because Zabían knew how to press every one of her buttons. Even the secret, hidden ones.

"You remember how to distinguish beech trees from black birches ?" she asked Zabían, who nodded with excitement. "Find me some chanterelles, little fox." His eyes lit up, and he scampered off.

"Mother, I think we're low on chaga," said Adelaida, her mouth unconsciously curling with distaste merely at the thought of the bitter, but very healthy, fungus. "Cook will never let me hear the end of it if I don't find some."

There was more tiredness in her tone than Lebía would have liked. "Oh, don't worry about that, love. I know you wanted time to yourself today. There's a lovely, low branch on that oak over there. Go ahead, I know you want to climb it. Just keep half an eye out for your brother."

Adelaida's face lit up, though she tried very hard to prevent that light from spilling into a smile. *There is so much of Voran in her.* But that was a dark thought, so Lebía carefully stowed it in a shadowy corner of her heart, to examine later.

"Thank you, Mother," Adelaida said, already skipping away. She *was* still a girl, for all the terrible seriousness of her nineteen years.

Draping her wicker basket over her left arm, Lebía wrapped herself in sunlight, loam-smell, and her shawl. They had passed a lovely stand of birches when they passed the river. There was sure to be chaga there.

And so it was—a rock-sized explosion of dark brown. It was a bit high for Lebía, but she could just reach it if she stood on a rock. There was one just nearby, so she put her weight on it. At the very last moment, she noticed a strip of green, and her mind said *algae,* just as her legs flailed out from under her. Instinctively, she reached down with her hand to stop her fall, but it slipped too. She landed elbow-first on a jagged shard of shale. The pain lanced upward, and her head spun.

Everything blurred in her vision, as though she were in two places at the same time. She closed her eyes, but that was worse. The ground spun underneath her. She snapped her eyes open, breathing deeply to prevent the wave of nausea from throttling her. Suddenly, she realized she was completely wet.

She was no longer on the bank near the birches, but at the exact point where two rivers flowed into one. Awkwardly, she stood up, knee-deep in foaming, icy water. She recognized this place—it was on the other side of the island, where the two rivers of Ghavan Isle met and emptied into the sea. Ahead of her, the combined torrent roiled, pierced through with irregular boulders, crooked as a giant's broken teeth.

About half a good bowshot away, Lebía saw something impossible.

The river simply ended, or melted away, or ceased to be, exactly at a point where the world itself seemed to bend upward and curve toward the sky. It was an almost transparent wall. Just as if Lebía were looking at a very large and transparent egg from the inside out. In the distance, at the far edge of the eggshell, where the blue of the sky darkened, something shimmered like waves.

On the other side of the transparent eggshell lay a dead Sirin.

Lebía half-crawled, half-trudged out of the water toward the left bank. She tripped every third step, but eventually came to the place where a shimmering, wave-like barrier stood between her and the dead Sirin. She reached out to touch it, but the Sirin's face stopped her. Lebía *knew* her, but she had forgotten the Sirin's name. Fair-haired, she was before. Not now. Now the gold was tainted with mud and blood. She had had gem-toned wings, like emerald with a light of its own, independent of the sun's shining. But not now. Now it was as though the Sirin's wings had wilted with the fall. And her face. Had it been beautiful? Surely it had. The stories were all of one accord—the Sirin were a beautiful race, their women's faces like statues brought to life by a poet's imagination.

How sad that no Sirin ever visited Ghavan, thought Lebía.

Lebía reeled. The world blinked out of existence, then reasserted itself. She was leaning against the birch again, reaching for the chaga.

She turned around in a panic, but there was no sign of the eggshell or the dead Sirin.

Something snapped in her mind, like a remembrance of a dream within a dream.

Had she ever seen any Sirin? No, surely not. There were no Sirin on Ghavan Isle. There had never been Sirin on Ghavan Isle.

"Mother!"

Lebía turned around, smiling. She was still astounded at how Zabían's squeaky five-year-old voice could force her to smile, even when she was tired and out of sorts.

"Look!" he said, through a torrent of giggles. He held a full bucket of chanterelles, or so he *thought* they were. Even from this distance, she could see that most of them were poisonous faux-chanterelles. Little foxes, the locals called them.

She turned back around again, expecting to see... Something. She had forgotten what. Had she seen something there just now? A creature of some kind? Something very sad? No. Just a remembrance of a dream within a dream. She turned back to her baby boy.

"Darling, I think you should let Adelaida check those for you first."

His entire body sagged, and his eyes looked ready to burst into tears.

Lebía laughed. "We'll make a mushroom-picker of you yet, my dear."

That snapping again. She had forgotten something vitally important. But what was it?

ఒుఞ

Lebía carried Zabían all the way back home for old times' sake, with Adelaida tutting quietly behind them. He was getting heavier by the hour, not the day.

At the threshold of their white-stone cottage—*this* was truly her home, not the three-story wooden monstrosity on the hill of the Dar—her other two daughters waited. The fourteen-year-old twins Marinka and Kachinka shone in jewel-bright blue and green wool dresses—*how did they get manage to keep that color so vivid, even after so many washes?* —nearly eclipsing Adelaida's faded brown homespun. Marinka's smile was so bright, it was almost a caricature. Kachinka's frown—she had probably just been berated for eating too many sweets again—was like her sister's smile, but turned upside down.

Someone was missing, though.

"Where's...?" began Lebía. She stopped, confused by the sudden disappearance of what she wanted to say from her mind.

"Father's with the carpenters preparing the last inserts for the rose window," said Adelaida, still glaring at Zabían, who had by now found something immensely fascinating in Lebía's left armpit. It tickled terribly, but Adelaida was wearing her extra-serious face again. Her eyes were eloquent in their demand that Lebía *not* act like a child. Even though Lebía thought she would explode with the effort of not laughing.

"No, not Mirnían, dear. I meant..." Who did she mean? "I don't even know." She chuckled, and the floodgates of laughter opened. "Zabían! You know I can't handle it..." She exploded into guffaws, her whole body shaking from Zabían's now deliberate tickle, as though he were a curious fox convinced there was a mouse hiding under her arm. She dropped him, as gently as she could, onto the grass.

The twins, now both smiling with very dangerous mischief, pounced on Lebía, picking up where Zabían left off.

"No, no, get off, get off!" Lebía huffed between spasms of alternating laughter and breathing. "Not...No! Adelaida, help!"

A very expertly-placed hand, with long-trained fingers, caught Lebía in the worst possible place—the back of her neck. Adelaida had betrayed her.

"Traitor!" Lebía managed to get out before dissolving into tearful giggles. She did the only thing she could—knees tucked up to her chest, arms protecting her head. They couldn't get at her that way.

The glow of the children's shared joy at torturing their mother was almost enough to counter the blaze of the sun setting over Aspen Hill.

"Well, the old ones do say that wet grass is uncommonly good for the constitution," said Mirnían's voice somewhere above Lebía. "Especially in the waning days of autumn. Soaking up Living Water for the winter, are we?" His forced seriousness could barely hold back the roar of laughter that was threatening to explode out of his flaring nostrils and dancing eyes.

"Husband!" Lebía called with mock severity from the ground. "Call the Dar's Guards! I've been attacked by vicious creatures of the wild! Beasts of legend, I tell you!"

All five of the children laughed.

No, not five. There were only four. Why had she thought there were five?

"Dinner, O mad rulers of Ghavan!"

Everyone fell silent instantly. The most feared person in all of Ghavan Isle, the cook Yeda, stood on the threshold, brandishing a wooden ladle the size of a small pony.

"You've done it now," whispered Kachinka at Zabían. "She'll never let us have those baked apples now."

"Do you ever think of anything but your stomach?" Marinka

raised her eyebrow significantly. Her ability to do that, as well as her slightly thinner face and figure, made the twins easy to tell apart. "Maybe you should think of your double chin instead." Kachinka pursed her lips and slitted her eyes. She said nothing, but Lebía had no doubt that a great deal of angry information was transmitted to her twin in their own special way of communicating. Marinka's raised eyebrow didn't so much as twitch the entire time.

"Come on then!" Lebía ushered them into the candle-lit anteroom. It already smelled of pork and cherries and mulled wine.

It was going to be a wonderful dinner. If only they could *all* be here for it...

"What just went through your head, my love?" asked Mirnían. "I've never seen your face turn so quickly from red to white to red again. Well, not since our wedding night, that is." He chuckled as she punched him in the stomach before pushing him into the dining room.

She stayed back, taking off her fur-lined kaftan more slowly than usual, trying to force calm on a heart that was doing its best to beat her rib cage down like an escaping prisoner. She had just seen an image, vivid as memory, in her mind's eye—the pale, dead face of a young man lying on the bank of a river that seemed to be on fire. A young man who had her face, whose name she knew better than her own. A son named Antomír. A son she had never had.

Or had she?

CHAPTER 2
THE VISION

T he next morning, ice encased the turning leaves as they fell, like a prophecy of snow. Lebía knew—down to the marrow in her bones—that the change had come. It was the first day of winter. Excitement and dread together—that was the telltale sign of the first day. Excitement for the low golden sun of winter, for the warmth of the hearth and the long hours of evening storytelling by the fire. The dread was for the coming night. In winter, even the vile powers who surrounded Ghavan were driven underground. They never went quietly—Winter's Night was always a storm of horrific wails and groans from the monsters who clawed at Adonais's protective girdle for the last time before being snowed under for the winter.

Lebía was the first to wake as always, careful not to disturb Mirnían. She knew, after many years of connubial bliss, that the early morning sleep was sweetest for him. She preferred to be up with the sun, and she had come to treasure the hour or so she had to herself, before the house of the Dar erupted in sounds of childish exuberance. This night, Zabían had stayed in his own bed in the children's room for once, so she felt rested as she had not in years. For once, the tendrils of fog embracing the fir trees outside the window were not mirrored by a fog in her head.

Lebía tiptoed out into the hearth-room, a rough square in the middle of the house, with four carved pillars holding up a roof with a small hole for the smoke. In the dance of firelight, the capitals extending out from the pillar-top onto the ceilings— masterfully carved Sirin's heads—seemed to wink at her playfully. Though that was a strange thought. She had not known any Sirin, but she was sure they were anything but playful.

Yeda had already been up for hours probably, knowing her. *Did she even sleep?* The daily pot of tea bubbled over the small hearth-fire, already spicing the air with clove and cinnamon. Lebía shivered with mixed pleasure and cold. Wrapping herself in her old woolen shawl, she poured the tea into her personal earthen cup—the one with the uneven lip. She loved its imperfection, its crookedness—at least a small something on Ghavan that wasn't ideal. Although no one believed her, she was sure that tea tasted much better in her cup than in any other.

Wrapped in both the aroma of the tea and the warmth of the shawl, she sat down on her rocking chair—a replica of her father Otchigen's favorite chair from Vasyllia. It was the only true connection she still had to the memory of her parents, and she cherished it like a secret love. No one seemed to remember anything of Otchigen except his madness and his supposed treachery, and even that was more a rumor and a series of tales than any clearly recalled events. She held one or two images of him near her heart, but it was the feeling of his bulk—a coziness like a mother bear—that overcame her whenever she sat in the chair and gently rocked, trying to avoid the inevitable creaking.

She hardly noticed the tears until they dripped into her tea.

"Why the tears, love?"

From behind the chair, Mirnían reached over the back of the chair, one hand caressing her cheek. She leaned against his arm, which was still hard with muscle, despite the long time of peace.

"I miss them, that's all. Father and Mother, and Voran especially."

Just the thought of him was enough for her eyes to seek out the last thing that remained of his memory—the now-famous sword of his mentor Tarin the Warrior-Storyteller, the sword Aglaia had jokingly called the Sword of the Raven Son. The strange feather-fire amalgam on its pommel caught the red of the hearth-fire more brightly than the rest of the blade, which was in need of a cleaning, not to mention a good smith for the several notches that remained.

"I'm sorry," she continued, "that you and he had no chance at reconciliation." In the first years after his death, that had weighed heavily on her.

"Why do you think I haven't taken the notches out?" he said, his voice cracking with emotion. "I look at that sword every day as a reminder of what I failed to do."

He was right. There was a certain justice to keeping it as it came to them. Voran's heroic death with this sword in his hands, his sacrifice bringing down both the Raven in Vasyllia and the city itself.

Mirnían had begun to sing:

"With sword's last strike, the Raven fell
As earth-bound fires consumed the land,
To doleful tolls of Vasyllia's bell."

"Oh, you know how much I hate that song!"

The now-ubiquitous *Ballad of the Raven Son*, especially the terrible last lines--everyone sang it. Mirnían chuckled, but the pain was still there—a pain she had tried to balm, but there was no miraculous cure for this wound.

"I know you do. I'm not crazy about it, either. But it does ensure that no one will ever forget Voran's sacrifice."

Lebía tried to imagine the scene—how Voran led the combined armies of Nebesta and Karila in battle against the Fallen in Vasyllia, how the Changers decimated the ranks of the Faithful, how it took the Pilgrim's own life to bring down the walls, and Voran's blood to cleanse the land of the foulness of the Raven...

And how Mirnían remained on Ghavan, nursing his fear. *You're doing it again*, she rebuked herself. Painting a mental icon of a hero that had little semblance to the living, breathing, often selfish, always thick-headed brother of hers. And painting a corresponding belittling picture of her own husband...

"His sacrifice," she said, musing. "Do you know? I still have no memory of his burial."

Everyone assured her that she had held him in her arms moments before he was interred in what was now called Aspen Hill. She remembered none of it.

"It was just the shock of seeing him dead, my dear. You never did have a chance to say goodbye properly."

He always said that. She had always believed him without thinking. But today, for some reason, she doubted.

What if it didn't actually happen?

As though she had summoned it with magic, the image of her never-born son Antomír flashed on her mind. He lay on the banks of a river on fire, his eyes glazed over...

Which is the real memory?

She shivered. The specter that sometimes haunted her steps, even in the perfection of Ghavan, loomed over her. And a rare memory from childhood surfaced: her father Otchigen, lying on the floor with his knees tucked up to his chest, gibbering madly and crying like a small child.

No. I will not go mad. I will not follow in Otchigen's footsteps.

As if a madwoman could stop her own madness.

"Well, if I had a silver penny to pay for *those* thoughts," said Mirnían, cupping her chin and shaking it gently. She melted at that familiar gesture.

"I'm sorry, love. It's been a strange few days."

But she couldn't quite remember why they were so strange. Something to do with... was it Sirin?...

The wind howled, and with it came the first heart-piercing

cry of the vila. Despite the fall of the Raven, not all his creatures had been destroyed. Most, attracted by the perfection of Ghavan, lingered at its edges, always trying to get in to wreak some final havoc before their miserable lives ended with the fading of the Raven's dark grace. It was why the protection around Ghavan remained, even now.

Though many years had passed, Lebía had to stop herself from running outside to answer the cry of the vila, that begging wail that seemed to come from hellish agony. She reminded herself—it was nothing more than a perfect lie, as were all the ruses of their other compatriots in monstrosity.

"It's beginning," said Mirnían. "It worked out perfectly, don't you think?"

She felt her eyebrows drawing together as she tried to understand what he was talking about. She turned her head back to see him, still standing behind her. His half-smirk was only partly hidden. She'd remind him of his husbandly duty to never point out her absentmindedness, or any other faults, later.

"The chapel, my swanling," he explained. "Today we're finishing the window."

How could she have forgotten? Ghavan's common work—the temple to Adonais on top of Voran's grave at Aspen Hill—was almost done. All they had to do was put in the rose window.

"Heights above, Mirnían! The procession. It's going to begin soon, and the children are all asleep!"

৩৫৩

It took all the children, even Adelaida, a maddeningly long time to get ready for the procession. Lebía already heard the rising waves of children's laughter and adults' annoyed shushing as the villagers passed the gate leading to the Dar's property. They always seemed to think it necessary to maintain reverent silence as they passed, as though the carved twin serpent-heads crowning the image of the sapling in bloom above the gate would come alive and bite them if their children were too loud.

"Marinka, not *those* temple rings, dear. Remember?" The silly child had chosen the ones with mermaids. Of *all* days.

"Zabían, are you sure you can manage carrying the banner?" She had been having visions of the triangular banner with the image of Voran's bloodied sword getting stuck in the leafless trees, as little Zabían singlehandedly tried to push back the tide of the procession to untangle it. It was worse than those dreams she sometimes had of appearing at village feasts naked.

"Kachinka, if you eat one more candied almond..."

Both twins giggled as they wrapped their heads in scarves and carefully attached their temple-rings. The right ones, this time. Simple sunbursts with an accent of moon crescent. Exactly right.

"Don't forget about yourself, my love," said Mirnían from the courtyard, already in his fur-lined hat and knee-length blue kaftan. He had worn the red boots, she noticed with a smile that made the pit of her stomach glow. She knew how much he hated them, even though all the women always noticed how kingly they looked. She'd reward him later. Then she realized she hadn't even begun doing her hair, and at least three wide-eyed village children were gaping at her from beyond the gate. They had never seen her head uncovered.

Oh, Heights! Why can't they just dress themselves, like normal children?

By the time everyone was ready, the trickle of people walking the cobbled road outside the gate was a steady stream. Mirnían wore that slightly exasperated look of the long-suffering husband.

No, I don't think I'll reward him after all.

The twins in their shambling gait and excessive giggling were doing their utmost best to suggest that they were adopted from a fisherman's family. Adelaida pranced next to Zabían on her tiptoes, her whole body like a bowstring ready to release. Lebía realized Adelaida was just as worried about the trees as she was. Zabían's irrepressible tongue stuck out, as it always did when he was concentrating too hard. His hands and arms shook with tension, but his back was as straight as his father's as he tried with every movement to imitate the perfection of his father's form and manner.

For a moment, something like a song sounded in her head as she breathed out the ecstasy filling her in swelling heart, tingling back, and dampening eyes. The conclusion of the twenty-year-long building of the temple felt like the logical conclusion to the saga of Vasyllia's fall and rise. The journey to this moment may have been fraught with dangers, but it was all worth it. Ghavan truly was a paradise, and she was a truly happy woman.

They joined the throng cresting the hill of the Dar's palace and down into the village proper. All the houses in the village were festooned with garlands of autumn leaves and rowan berries, and some of the more enthusiastic of the ladies had thrown ribbons of all colors across the gap between the houses in the central street of the village. Smells of fish guts and tanning of skins—always prevalent in this busiest part of Ghavan Town —were overwhelmed by the sour, pleasant aroma of fermenting cabbage. The air itself seemed to breathe out the essence of freshly-baked bread. Lebía imagined the cracking of the ceremonial loaf in her hands. She and Mirnían would be the first to salt, then partake of, Winter's Loaf.

"Mother, look at that silly boy!" Zabían said to her, pointing with his nose, as his hands were still busy in the important business of not dropping the banner.

It was the baker's son, who should have been with the children leading the procession, each carrying their own carved or painted image of a High Being.

"He's sick, the poor boy," said Lebía dreamily, not quite sure how she knew that. The baker's wife must have told her. "Nothing serious, of course." No one was ever sick for long on Ghavan. "He'll be all right in a day or two."

A strange, tingling pain crawled up her right palm. Then a sharp, piercing shock, as of a long splinter. She almost yelped in surprise as she looked at her hand. There was nothing there.

She blinked, and the world reeled around her for a split second, echoing itself countless times like the repeated images in a broken mirror. Then everything was normal again.

Her heart shuddering in her chest, Lebía jerked her head up to look at the boy. She knew, somehow, that he was about to hurt himself on the windowsill, which had a long splinter of wood just underneath the window. She didn't suspect it. She knew it. As though... *as though it had happened before.*

The boy, entranced by the three leading banners held by Otar Yustav and his two acolytes, slipped. His body toppled halfway out of the window as he tried to stop himself with his outstretched palms. The long splinter nearly impaled his right hand.

His yelp was enough to drown out even the people's singing of the traditional pilgrim songs.

Poor little cub, she thought. *Where's his mother, anyway?*

"Poor little cub," said Mirnían, "Where's his mother, anyway?"

Lebía's face grew cold as the blood drained from it. Had he read her mind? No. *She* had known what he was going to say before he said it.

She turned to look at the twins.

They are about to throw a carefully prepared mud-ice ball at Iziaslava, the carpenter's wife. And she's going to turn her head to the right and the left, then pretend it didn't happen.

Kachinka, whispering in conspiratorial half-phrases intelligible to no one but her twin, pulled out a large, hailstone-sized concoction of mud and ice from under Marinka's cloak and threw it at Iziaslava, who had earned the ire of both twins when she stopped providing them with dumplings every morning behind Lebía's back. The mud ball hit her in the small of her back, making a painful thud that Lebía anticipated by the shrug-

ging of her own shoulders. Iziaslava turned her head to the right
and the left, then pretended it didn't happen.

No, it can't be, Lebía told herself. *It's just the smallness of the
village. It's just that I know them all so well. I just guessed.*
The hopefulness of the lie did little to reassure her.

What was happening to her? First the images of a never-born
son, now this strange prescience? None of it made any sense.

"My love, you'd better hurry if you don't want to be the *last*
person to have the Winter Loaf," whispered Mirnían with more
than a little irritation in his voice. They were crossing past the
last house of the village into the welcome embrace and cool,
scented air of the pine trees. She looked at him. His eyes
widened at her expression. Judging by his face, it seemed that
she was looking at him as though she didn't know him. She tried
to smile.

"No, don't do that," he said, grimacing. "If you don't feel
yourself, don't pretend. You were never good at that false smile. I
prefer you as you are." His voice seemed more, not less, irritated,
though.

Don't blame me for your own dislike of public events, she thought.
It was a strange thought.

"Don't blame mother for your dislike of public events,
father," said Adelaida, her secret joy spilling out from her eye-
crinkles and the edges of her half-smile.

Though the shock prevented Lebía from speaking, she still
had the presence of mind to thank Adelaida for always being the
one to gently pull Mirnían back to his better self.

That thought was an anchor. She may be going mad in some
previously unheard-of way, but *this* was real. This child of theirs,
this product of their love. She was as real as anything that Lebía
had ever experienced. And it was enough to know that she *was.*

But what about my son Antomír? Is he real?
For the rest of the procession, nothing strange happened.

The single cobbled road in Ghavan Isle meandered through the firs encircling the village. As the road rose slightly, it straightened until it reached a point where the hills seemed to part for it. Wrought iron lanterns, each with a unique design in fancies of flora and fauna, lined this road, and it continued straight until a sharp incline to the top of a hillock crowned with orange-leaved aspens. The trees grew in clumps, forming a rough circle around a white stone temple with three towers. Each tower had a gable, oddly made out of stacked logs in the old Nebesti fashion, painted in gold and silver. Each gable was topped with a carved, unpainted figure in now-weathered wood. The first figure was a falcon in flight—the symbol most people associated with Voran. The second was a loping wolf—Aglaia in her final form. The third was the snarling maw of a bear.

Lebía still found it ironic that the bear should be a symbol of Mirnían's Darship. He had very little of the bear in him, nor had he ever needed to find that ferocity within himself. Voran had done all the work. Mirnían had never even left the island.

With a lurch of her heart in her chest, she berated herself for so easily thinking ill of her husband. Twice in one day!

"I know," said Mirnían, making her jump. "I don't like it either. But you can hardly blame them. Or me, I hope."

Had he been reading her mind?

"No, I didn't read your thoughts, my love," he said, laughing like a boy in that rare chuckle she liked so much. "You're just very easy to read. To me, at least."

He shrugged his shoulders as his cheeks reddened a bit. He looked down. She wanted to hug him fiercely as motherly affection warred with passionate love, like two waves cresting at the same moment in a cross-current.

The banners had just reached the point of ascent on the road. The mood of the crowd shifted from boisterous to hushed. A few still sang, but they were the elders, given permission to sing on hallowed ground. Even the children knew to restrain themselves. Even her twins walked a little straighter, giggled a little less.

As she ascended, she felt a twinge of resentment simmering under the waves of affection she had just felt for Mirnían. He could have been a better Dar, she knew. But he had never grown to his full stature. He was always content to remain with the Faithful on Ghavan, leaving the restoration of the Three Lands to those outside, to Regent Sabíana, whom she hadn't seen at all since Vasyllia, and to others she didn't know. People said Sabíana had become hard and sharp, like tempered steel, in her role as rebuilder of the world burned by the Raven. Lebía could imagine it. There was always something hard about Sabíana, for all she loved Voran deeply.

The three banners arrived at the crest of Aspen Hill just as the sun reached its zenith. The golden threads woven into the burgundy felt of the banners sparkled like ice crystals on the air of a winter's morning. Even the smallest of the children gasped. Zabían didn't even look up, his eyes trying to find another outlet through the top of his head as he struggled to keep his face forward and also make sure the banner remained high and straight. Mirnían grazed the small of her back with his hand, partly to help her up the hill, but partly as one of his many small, seemingly insignificant gestures that no one else noticed, but that she prized higher than gold. She leaned into him with more force than he expected, making him stop off the road for a second. He chuckled into her headscarf, making her blush.

The children surrounded the temple and pulled out their festal bells from under their kaftans, waiting for Otar Yustav's signal. He prostrated himself three times before the door of the temple, which was open, then turned to face the people. He bowed to his waist, then extended his hands up and outward, so that the sun seemed to pour its rays down on him as into a living goblet. The children rang and rang and rang their bells, giving vent to their delight with their whooping and their laughter.

"Our brother and lord, the exiled warrior and the beloved of the Regent Sabíana, Voran the son of Otchigen of Vasyllia, awarded posthumously the old title of Voyevoda and Judge of the Mother of Cities..."

Otar Yustav, though a small man of wiry muscle and hard angles, had a voice like all the songbirds on the first day of spring.

"...His sacrifice it was that ended the Raven's baneful lordship over the Mother of Cities. His blood it was that washed the blighted earth clean. It was fitting. A sacrifice to end all sacrifices. And today, we dedicate this temple to the memory of the one he served. The Pilgrim's Haven, this place will be called. A haven for all who come to Ghavan Isle to rest their wearied bodies and souls."

"So be it!" Called the warriors, though there were few enough of them left.

"So be it!" called the villagers, many of whom wept openly.

"SOBEIT!" cried the children, as if it were a single word of power, not three.

"Enter, brothers and sisters, enter!"

The temple was spacious, with ribbed vaults flying up from the marble floor like swiftly-growing trees. The vaulting met at the center along a single wooden beam, from which hung bunches of mistletoe, rowan berries, and wilting aspen branches, their orange still bright, even in the gloom of candlelight. Tall, narrow windows allowed just enough light to see, though the space was dim enough to seem not of this world, as though it were an opening into a Realm of Aer somewhere in the clouds. The smoking censers hanging on the walls intensified the effect.

Lebía hadn't seen it for a year, like everyone else in the village. It was like seeing it for the first time. Although none of it looked like anything in Vasyllia, memories of Voran inundated her as they always did. A field of tall grass, waving with the hidden form of her thirteen-year-old brother as he tried to sneak up on her and Sabíana in secret. Voran, fifteen years old, in the fighters' pentagon of the seminary, methodically and coldly destroying the inept attacks of every other boy in his cohort. That infuriating half-smile—it even made *her* want to try her luck against him in battle. That hollowness inside his eyes the day he heard about the massacre of the Karilan embassy, his inner grief fractured because of his loss and his need to be a protector to her.

The tears gathered, blurring her vision. She struggled to breathe. Between breaths, her chest heaved, and she couldn't stop the sobs from hiccuping out of her. Embarrassing. As though she were some drunk wandering the back alleys of Vasyllia's first reach.

By the time she stilled the sobbing enough for it to be a mere ache, not a storm, two ladders had been set up over the altar area, where a hole gaped in the stone wall. The last piece of this edifice, built by the hands of Ghavan's villagers—all of them—one stone at a time, one procession at a time. The window, apparently a miracle of colored glass set in a secret design of wrought iron, was the work of one man.

She remembered the day the artisan had come—a cold spring morning twenty years ago. He had given no name as he arrived on Ghavan with the last of the refugees. Among the many wounded from the wars, he had been almost inconspicuous in his grey cloak, his face nondescript, as though hiding behind a beard that was more bush than human hair. He had not spoken more than two words to anyone over those twenty years, but he never closed the door to his workshop. People came at all hours to see the marvels he created. In the last year, he had focused all his attention on this window. Lebía had come a few times herself, but at close quarters, she didn't understand the design. It seemed abstract. When she asked him about it, he looked at her with eyes that reminded her of someone from a long time ago, but he had said nothing to her, nor to anyone, about what he was planning.

Now they would all know what the strange artisan had been crafting all these years.

It took five men to carry the window, another four to hold the ladders steady. Whether they had planned it so or not, Lebía suspected that the sun would shine exactly through that window in no more than a half hour. She hoped they would manage to install it in time. An expectant silence extended out from the working men like a blanket. Mothers embraced their children, and Lebía couldn't decide whose eyes were more childishly expectant. Many fathers' eyes glistened with unshed tears. The old men nodded to each other in appreciation, while their wives tapped on their shoulders to be still.

With a final groan and a sprinkling of stone dust that made half the builders sneeze, the window was installed. First whispers, then hushed murmurs passed through the people, growing louder and louder. Lebía couldn't tear her eyes away from the image. The colors glowed as though they were providing the light *for* the sun, not the other way around. The hues shifted, as though the image was moving. Her shoulders tensed; her elbows creaked under the strain. Her jaw pulsed as she ground her teeth together, the pain lancing her to the bones of her skull.

The image, glowing in colors so bright no Vasylli had the language to express them, was of a tree. A sapling of white bark and round, translucent leaves. White bunches of flowers, like grapes, hung from the branches. She could almost smell them— tuberose and lavender and orange teased her senses. Then the sun broke the plane of the outer edge of wrought iron, and the leaves burst into flame. Her mind tried to tell her that they were orange bits of glass that had not caught the light of the direct sun until that moment. That it was merely the mastery of the silent artisan. But her heart refused to listen.

For she knew that sapling. She had not thought of that tree for... twenty years. No. She had forgotten all about it. Everyone had. It was once called the Covenant Tree, and it had stood in the center of Ghavan until... until... until...

Lebía screamed.

She remembered. A cloud of formless shapes, myriad eyes

glinting inside it as it spun in a vortex over the island known as Ghavan. A tree aflame with Sirin flying around it, weeping tears of opalescent glimmer. The Sirin falling to the ground as the flames guttered and died. With the fall of the Sirin, a tidal wave rose all around the island, rising up, up, up as the entire village, the entire island, fell into the waters of the Great Sea. A boat on that wave, flying away... no, floating up, up, remaining on top of the tidal wave as the rest of them sank to another Realm. In that boat was a young man with golden hair and eyes like the sky after a storm. His arms reached down to her.

"Mother!" he had cried. Antomír. Her son.

She fell, hard, as though the earth opened up beneath her. She snapped awake.

CHAPTER 3
THE ARTISAN

Lebía stood under a sweeping maple-canopy, its leaves rust-red, on the shore of a river running between two hills before emptying into the Great Sea. She remembered this place as a regular stopping point in her daily walks from Ghavan to the Sea twenty years ago. This was before Mirnían had returned, when Antomír was only a baby. She hadn't stepped foot in this place in...

The pain was like a wedge splitting a log, but aimed right between her eyes.

She had two sets of memories, both equally vivid, but belonging to two lives that couldn't possibly have both happened. She saw herself walking with Antomír toward the sea in the morning. He was already sixteen at least. They chattered happily about how much she worried during those early days, how every morning she imagined Mirnían dying a new and more inventive death. But she also remembered that she had not come here in over twenty years. But that was impossible. If both things were true, then she would be around sixty years old. But her hands were the same as they were yesterday, her back was as straight as it was when the tree still grew in Ghavan, and she was sure she was no older than thirty-five, perhaps forty at the most.

Two lives, overlapped. Impossible to have lived both. And yet... she had... hadn't she?

She closed her eyes and put her head into her palms. The world spun around her, or rather she spun around it, with everything else being solid. Only she was a whirlwind with nothing to moor her to the earth.

"Took you long enough, Heights above!" said an unfamiliar voice, hacking a nasty cough between every few words. The voice belonged to a man with hair and beard so long and matted that he could easily pass for some long-forgotten spirit of the forest. His eyes bored into her, and she remembered them. It was the artisan. But older by many years.

She opened her mouth to ask the obvious question. He raised his hand before she had finished breathing in.

"Yes, yes, yes. Confusion and befuddlement. First, turn around and look."

She was more inclined to snap at him, but there was something very wrong with everything. So she did as she was told.

Just behind her was the same shimmering, transparent wall that had separated her from Aína's dead body. Only now, she saw Ghavan town in the distance, foggy and indistinct. She was on the *other side* of the eggshell.

The pain turned to panic. She leaned against the eggshell, pushing it, but it was cold and firm as tempered steel.

She turned back to the old man fiercely, this time breathing in advance so he could not stop her.

He still interrupted her. "Twenty years," he said.

She froze in mid-word. Then she felt her eyes widen in shock. She thought she understood.

Again, he anticipated her. "No. You understand nothing at all."

She wanted to slap him, but he had turned to face the transparent wall, touching it with a hand shriveled with age. The wall shimmered. The scene behind it shifted. She saw the streets of Ghavan filled with the forms of people who looked as though they had fallen asleep in mid-stride. The baker with his hands still in the dough. The potter with his foot stuck on the pedal, the turning wheel coming to a slow stop. Mirnían, leaning against the wall of the temple.

Except...

"You've killed them!" she exclaimed, pouncing on him and trying to throttle him before realizing what she was doing. She pushed him down as she stepped back. He got up slowly, hacking wildly all the time. He backed away from her as though she were a wild beast.

"If you have done anything to my..." she said in as imperious a tone as she could muster after twenty years—or however much it was—of being a Dar's wife.

"Do you know?" he complained, still huffing like a bellows. "That tone doesn't suit you. You were never the high and mighty type."

His nonchalance disarmed her enough that for a moment she had nothing to say.

He looked around for a rock or a log or something comfortable to sit on. But there was nothing but a few jagged rocks by the riverside. They were wet and mossy and looked slippery enough for him to slide right into the water as soon as he attempted it. So he remained standing. His expression made it very clear he considered her at fault for this situation.

"This is going to be miserable," he groaned. "It's all complicated enough, even without this old body with its creaking and its puffing and its..."

"Enough," she commanded calmly, but with an edge. "Speak."

He did.

༺✦༻

"Have you ever seen one of those automatons that wind up and play the same scene over and over again?"

Lebía understood perhaps one word in that sentence. His exasperated sigh made it clear he could see as much.

"Perhaps we should go even further back. To the moment you don't want to remember."

An iron chain seemed to squeeze her heart, but she balled her hands into fists and ground her teeth until her body pushed the scream away.

"It was quite a thing, I'll tell you. To see it from ..." He cleared his throat quickly, as though he had almost let something improper slip. "The Sirin who guarded this place truly had a force of love that I have never before seen. They almost performed an impossible feat—the full transfer of an entire island, with all its denizens, into a different Realm of Aer, from a place where there was, and is, no door to another Realm."

"Almost?" Her voice sounded choked.

"You really have no idea how difficult it is. What sort of power is needed. A Majestva could perhaps do it, even though I doubt it. But a Sirin? They're not High Beings at all, you know. Barely more than a beast with a voice and a mind. And yet, Aína by herself almost managed it. But she died before she could complete it."

Lebía's jaw ached from her teeth grinding. So she *had* seen Aína's body, after all.

"Ghavan Isle is stuck in a very strange place between the Realms, my Darina," the title he spoke with obvious sarcasm. "When it got stuck, all of you, every single Ghavanite, fell asleep. That gave me my first hint. This place was not quite the realm of sleep, not quite the realm of death. A place with elements of sleep and vision both. A very, very perilous realm. So I made my great creation. The egg."

As he talked, he shuffled back and forth, hoping that some place to sit would materialize out of thin air. Finally, he just collapsed in a heap on the ground and leaned against the transparent wall.

"The egg. Yes. An egg with a clockwork mechanism inside it,

a perfectly formed scene that plays itself out before the viewer in brilliant, miniature detail. A play, of sorts. With you characters in it."

"Speak plainly." Lebía barely got it out. She suspected something horrible was about to become clear. There was no time for this old man's silly asides.

"Every day of this year, I designed myself. It took a great deal of effort. Most of what happens is scripted, so to speak. But I put enough free will in there for the main characters. You. Mirnían. A few others."

A strange calm descended on her. It was a calm like death. "You... created... the life of my family. They didn't exist before the egg, I know that now. None of my children. They're all... are they dreams or illusions?"

"Ah, you're always jumping ahead! I'll get to that." He grumbled something irritated into his extensive bush-beard. "I had only enough skill to create a single year in the parallel Ghavan. This parallel world has a different history. All is peaceful. The Raven was defeated. Voran died, and a cult of reverence arose after his sacrifice. There was no Covenant Tree, and Sabíana ruled alone in a distant Vasyllia that no Ghavanite ever wanted to visit. Everyone had families and Ghavan continued to give its health and bounty. A veritable paradise, if I say so myself."

"But *why*?"

"I'm getting there. I entered that space myself and set everything up to give you or Mirnían the necessary... stimulus... to wake one of you up."

"But we didn't wake up."

"No," he almost growled. "You didn't."

Finally, she thought she understood the reason why the artisan looked middle-aged inside the egg, but like an old man outside it. A great deal of time had passed outside the egg, while everything inside remained stuck in a different time.

"I put all the strength I had left into the installation of the rose window. I had left you and Mirnían with a single memory, like a dream within a dream, of the real history of the world outside Ghavan. So when you looked at the mosaic of the Covenant Tree, it was supposed to be such a jarring experience for you or Mirnían, so out of touch with the apparent reality of your perfect life, that you were supposed to wake up, as from a nightmare."

"You invented my children, an entire society of people, and twenty years of a life shared in love and prosperity... all for a single moment of shock?"

The horror in her words didn't seem to register in his expression at all. "Except it didn't work. Neither you nor Mirnían woke up. Then something strange happened. Everything... started over from the first day, the year beginning from day one, extending toward the final day of the installation of the window. When the second year also failed to wake you up, the whole thing started over a third time."

Realization, or something approximating it, dawned on Lebía, but like a sunrise still wreathed in fog.

"That's how I knew what would happen at the procession. It had happened already."

"Twenty times, at least," he said. "Every year, the installation of the rose window made more and more of an impression on you. It never made any kind of impression on Mirnían at all. Then, this year, you finally snapped out of it."

His gaze was curious. He didn't want to ask her, but he wanted to know. She saw no reason to hide it from him. "I had a vision of Aína, dead, on the other side of the eggshell."

His eyes open so wide, it looked almost inhuman. "But... that never happened. Aína's body was taken back up to wherever it is the Sirin live as soon as she died. I built the egg later."

He was afraid. That thought unsettled her. He had been so sure of his creation, so sure of his complete mastery of this place. What else had slipped out of his control?

That thought forced her to look at him more carefully. The

throbbing in her head subsided and the tightness around her chest lightened a little.

"You're not human. So what are you?" she asked, genuinely interested.

The speed with which his head snapped in her direction was disconcerting. Like a strange mix of snake and bird. Definitely not human. And yet... he had lived among them, or a version of him had. And he had created an astounding work of art. A living world within a world that continued to exist and change and become more complex, even beyond its creator's plan. This artisan had created a thing of surpassing beauty. He was, in some small way, a surrogate parent to her own children.

But...

"You did all this for your own reasons, didn't you? Selfish ones, most likely, but I think you fell in love with a paradise of your own making."

The old man's face jerked toward her, and his eyes glowed for a moment as his features... shifted. Something wolfish passed over his face, then the old artisan reappeared.

"Yes," she said, more to herself than him. "As I thought. You're a changer."

He nodded, his posture like a caged animal backed into a corner.

With a flash of insight, she imagined what hell this changer must have lived in before he created an alternate Ghavan, a simulacrum of paradise. Of course he fell in love with it! It was *almost* real. She could almost forgive him...

But he gave me the likeness of a perfect life, then he took it all away from me. Why?

There had to be another reason why he had put so much effort into waking her. Then it hit her. She laughed, but it was the laugh of a convict told that she was about to eat her last meal before execution.

"Of course. It's all about Living Water, isn't it?"

His breathing grew raspy, and a hint of a growl rumbled in the back of his throat. "Yes."

"That's why you need me. You can't get the Living Water yourself, because of who you are."

His entire form rippled, but he remained in place.

Lebía was shocked to find that she felt sorry for the artisan.

"I will help you," she said, at which he cocked his head at her in surprise. "Perhaps. We may have to help each other, I think." The ache in her heart and the pounding in her head had reasserted itself, making it hard to think, much less speak. "But I need you to help me first. I need to understand. What is the truth of things outside Ghavan? In the real."

His eyes widened. "You want to know that? But I have been trapped in this in-between Realm as well."

"You have knowledge. Some, at least. Else, how could you have put the thought of Antomír's death into my mind?"

His face went white in genuine shock. "Death? What do you mean, death?"

So that memory wasn't one of his. The thought scared her, even as it gave her hope. She moved toward the changer, but he leaned back and bared a set of teeth that had suddenly grown fangs. He was something like an animal, after all. She had to think of him not as an artisan only, but also as a thinking animal. With a very strong instinct for self-preservation.

"Listen to me," she said, raising her hands placatingly. "The more I understand, the more we can help each other. You want to leave this place as much as I do, I assume."

Slowly, he nodded.

"Tell me about Vasyllia. The Raven. All of it."

A quickly-flashed smile, or more a bared maw, and Lebía had to physically restrain herself from jumping away and yelping.

"The Raven still has Vasyllia. Voran... he is alive. Or was, before I was trapped in here. But he was a changed man." The artisan chuckled, as though his pun wasn't intentional. "He had lost most of his hope. As for your son, Antomír, the last I knew, he was alive, that is, none of my brothers...you'd call them *changers*... had consumed him. I would have known that much, even here."

How little she knew about the changers, Lebía realized. Had they a nature that was complete enough in itself to allow for personal desires and wills, outside the will of the Raven? Could this creature ever be a... friend?

Surely not.

"So... things are much as they were then? But... what about time here, outside the egg? Has twenty years passed in the real as well?"

The changer looked away.

"You don't know, do you?"

He shook his head. His beard had been slowly gathering color, growing shorter and less matted as they spoke.

"What if I asked you to guess?"

The artisan again looked shocked, as though he never expected she would give him the benefit of the doubt.

"I don't think the Realm in which Ghavan is stuck is moved by time any more than the world inside the egg. I think that if we ever leave, it will be to return close to the time when we entered. But I don't know."

"All this uncertainty. All this waiting. And all for the Living Water? Why?"

Its form shifted without sound. And yet, the movement was like a groan of pain.

"You don't know," he said, groaning between phrases. "You could never know. To be formless... it is insatiable hunger. Living Water in the hands of the Raven... He has promised us all... permanent forms."

A wave of emotion struck Lebía in the pit of the stomach. "Will you tell me what you were, before your form was... taken from you?"

His eyes were almost all whites. A frightened animal. He was a predator, certainly, but as frightened of her as of a beast larger and more powerful than he.

"I was... a Majestva."

One of the higher Powers, she knew. An angelic being that often appeared as winds-made-visible with myriad eyes. Voran had once told her, many years ago, about a revolution in the Heights, a kind of power struggle between the Raven and his creator, during which many powers took the side of the Raven. She couldn't quite remember the details of it, but she did know that all those who followed the Raven had become changers— formless, shifting creatures always lusting after the permanence they used to have, but were now forever denied.

She looked at the pathetic figure crouched on the grass, and she was surprised by the tears that gathered in her eyes.

"You must have been... beautiful..."

His eyes remained huge, but the softness around his mouth tightened into a grimace. His nostrils flared as though he were having trouble breathing. Red color flooded his face.

Suddenly, something moved inside the egg, running swiftly toward the sleeping Mirnían. It wasn't a man-shape at all. It was a lynx with the younger face of the artisan who lived inside the egg, snarling insanely at Lebía through the shimmering wall. It pounced on top of Mirnían, both front paws lodged in Mirnían's neck. The claws were so deep inside his neck that she could no longer see them. Blood seeped from under the grey, speckled paws.

Lebía's whole body shook so hard that her teeth chattered. She could no longer stop it. She screamed.

"Shut up! Enough wasting time," hissed the old changer next to her. "Only you can save him now. Bring me Living Water, and I will not kill him."

A vila shrieked at Lebía's right. She jerked in that direction, shocked to see the sky suddenly black with roiling clouds over a small section of woods where she knew the Living Water was supposed to be located.

"But... you're not the only one?" she managed to say, through her shuddering jaw.

His smile was feral, the teeth still longer than normal in the fangs. "Oh, didn't I mention? Yes, there are some rather nasty beasties in that wood. They've all been trying to get at the Living Water for the last twenty years. No luck, though."

He extended his hand to her. A transparent egg, larger than a goose egg, lay in his palm. Inside, she saw a perfect likeness of Mirnían, sleeping peacefully on their shared bed in Ghavan town. A paper-thin scratch reached from his earlobe to his chin. A trickle of blood crept down his neck.

"That scratch," said the changer. "When it reaches all across his neck, then you'll know it's too late. He'll be dead. You have one hour."

CHAPTER 4
THE EGG

Greyish light, afflicted with mist, leaked through the spaces between the branches of trees that seemed to whisper dark curses at each other. Before, the susurration of the forest would have entranced Lebía, who loved to listen to the ancient songs of leaf and branch and bark, trying to puzzle out its meaning. But now, every creak, every rustle threatened her in an unknown tongue. This was Ghavan, she said to herself. But it wasn't the Ghavan she knew. It was a place poisoned and defiled by a creeping infection.

Lebía stood frozen in utter terror at the shadows between the trees, into which she would have rushed eagerly, seeking rest, only hours before. Here and there the mist seemed to coalesce in brief shapes that moved contrary to the wind. Vila, probably, or something worse. What could she possibly do against vila, with their razor sharp teeth and their ability to suck the life out of her, should they choose? What other monsters from legend would she find in the groves that used to be protected by Adonais's girdle of power? The earth itself seemed to growl underneath the vila's screams in a parody of harmony. Directly ahead of her, the moss-covered willows bordering the Ghavan River began to shake with a heavy wind. No, it was more than the wind. Some *thing* was shaking them.

Then she saw them—the *rusalkas* in the trees, their green hair waving around them as though they were underwater. The egg in her palm flashed suddenly. Mirnían's scratch had reached the edge of his Adam's apple.

The earth heaved under her feet. Gasping, she stumbled to one knee. The ground gathered around her feet like a shirt being tucked in, then it took her legs and threw her forward into the forest. A crevice gaped ahead of her. She fell straight into the river.

The cold water yawned to swallow her up. The breath in her lungs, frightened clean out of her chest, had no intention of coming back. As she tensed her whole body to push herself out to breathe, iron fingers grabbed her hair and thrust her head underwater.

No! Not rusalka! Not the drowned ones!

She pushed back, trying to grab at the thing that kept her underwater, but there seemed to be no one anywhere around her. Just a disembodied hand holding her head underwater.

Just as she thought her chest would explode from lack of air, something shoved her, as though she were an old door wedged in place by a rusted bolt. Spluttering and gasping for air, she pulled herself up by her nails, clinging to tree roots covered in slimy, lime-green algae. She turned back to see two *rusalkas* fighting each other on the bank. Their nails were already bloody. It seemed their greed had saved her. For the moment.

Lebía pushed up against the ground as her feet churned the mud. Half crawling, half running, she went deeper into the forest.

A shadow flitted between two pine trees—something horned and with hooves, but walking upright. The sight was enough to make her breath flee again. Lebía tried to find herself inside the panic.

This is real. This land. This haven. I am of it. Surely some of the old protection still remains!

Lebía's thoughts were jagged, almost not her own. But they were enough to force her upright.

She was running again. Nothing was going to stop her, even if she wasn't quite clear where the cave was, exactly. All that was left was the compulsion, Mirnían's pale face and the steady trickle of blood driving her forward.

A shape flew over her head, white and ragged like a ripped bedsheet. The song of the vila reached into her chest and tried to tear her heart out. This vila was all teeth—nothing but knife-teeth in a ghostly face, too long and pale to be human. The ground heaved under Lebía, the trees reaching down, not to grab, but to strike her down. Lebía fell to the ground, scrabbling the dirt as she tried to pull herself away from the three vila— there seemed nothing but teeth, nothing but teeth—as they swooped over her body. Their songs scratched at her from inside her chest. The dirt dug into her nails. Her palms glistened with blood when she turned them over.

Before she knew what she was doing, Lebía had a tree branch in her hand and she swung wildly at the vila, over and over again, until the shapes floated off and howled away into the mist creeping between the trees.

A horned shape resolved itself from the tree-shadows. She remembered what it was called from her nurse's childhood tales. A Leshiy— it had horns of a ram adorning a bearded face with a third horn coming out of its forehead. Its dirt-brown fur dripped from the noxious mist. Moss clung to the fur all the way to its goat-hooves. The six fingers of each hand were tipped with razor-sharp nails.

It snarled, exposing two rows of sharp teeth. The growl coming from it seemed to come from underneath the earth. It promised not mere death, but pain. A lot of pain.

Lebía ran, conscious that her legs were gouged from running

through brush. Something slashed across her back. Fire-pain laced across her shoulder blades.

No, I will not stop.

Now, four horned Leshiy blocked her way. One of them brandished a tree stump. It ran at her, with the three others running after it, roaring. Terror overwhelmed her. She turned to avoid them, running, she was hoping, generally in the direction of the cave with the Living Water.

She felt the breath of the monsters almost on her neck. It stank. The voice was inside her head even before she heard it through the creaking of the trees and the wind rushing through the leaves.

"Go on," it growled, mocking. "It is ours now. We will not share it."

Lebía tripped on a tree root, just before realizing that what she thought was a slight dip in the forest floor was the edge of a rock face. She fell down it, head over feet, until she felt her head stop against something hard. Everything kept spinning...

She blinked.

She was sitting on leaf-mold, her back against a boulder that loomed over her. The air itself seemed to be pausing between breaths.

She must have passed out from the fear.

How much time do I have left?

She looked at the egg in her hand. It was covered in blood, sitting on a palm that looked more like ground meat than a human hand. She scrabbled at it, trying to wipe it off just enough to see... the red line was almost at his right ear...

Something seemed to stab at her neck. She reached for it, but her left arm could only rise so far. It was probably dislocated, if not broken. She licked her lips, sensing blood pouring from somewhere on her face. They were salty with caked blood. She shifted her weight, and nearly screamed. Her legs tore agony through her body every time she tried to move.

I'm broken, she thought. *I'm going to die here.*

She looked around. The place was familiar. Whether it was chance or some leftover of Aína's grace, just in front of her was the cave with the Living Water. None of the Leshiy were there. But she felt, on the level of instinct, that they were waiting in the shadows. Why didn't they just finish her off?

"Go on," the wind whispered.

Except it wasn't the wind. It was something that looked like a human being distorted to the height of a tree. Grey skin stretched over sharp skull-bones. Branch-like hands extended from a body wreathed in a robe that looked like moss-covered bark. Hair like slugs framed a grey face with jowls sagging to either side of a single eye socket with a red-rimmed eye. She recognized it from her Vasylli childhood. That was the Likho, the one-eyed reaper of souls. All the worst nightmares of Vasylli children made flesh.

"I will help you," the Likho breathed in a voice like winter cracking dead leaves. She pulled Lebía's body forward with her crooked hands. Lebía pushed back against the soft earth with her half-dead legs, but they gave way, inch by inch. Something hard caught at her ribs with every breath.

Please, please, no!

It was pitch-black inside the cave. As her eyes grew used to the darkness, the skin on her neck curdled. Something was wrong: the smell. It was like twenty years' worth of carrion heaped in a single place.

All around the pool of Living Water, sticks were driven into the soft earth. On top of each was an animal skull. Lebía saw the place where the water used to be. There was nothing there but a dry clay bed. There had not been any water there in years.

"Likho, is that you?" wheezed a voice echoing as though the walls themselves had hundreds of mouths, all speaking in unison.

Lebía raised her eyes to see a huge head lodged in the ground of the cave, aligned with the mass of the back wall where the pool of Living Water used to be. Its hair was the roots of trees that grew in the ground above their heads. Its face was no different from muddy rock. Its eyes... It had no eyes.

But she was wrong. It did have eyes. They were stuck to the ends of eye-stalks that fell all the way to the ground and could not lift themselves up.

She had never even heard of such a monstrosity.

The vila shrieked as they flew into the cave and circled Lebía, coming closer and closer. Even in the half-murk, their teeth glittered. The Leshiy stood at the mouth of the cave, intent on keeping her in. Two of them walked up to the head, sidestepping Lebía, and lifted the huge eyelids, until two massive slitted cats' eyes stared at her.

Lebía fell to the ground, filled to the brim with terror, disgust, and despair.

"Good," the head wheezed as Likho approached it and turned to face Lebía. "This one is full of joys and sorrows. Full of a life lived. We will gorge ourselves on this one."

"The agreement!" hissed one of the Leshiy.

"Yes, I do not forget. We take her spirit only. Her body is yours to feast upon. You have not had human flesh in years, I think."

Something glimmered in the cave—a light of pale, shimmering gold. It was coming from Lebía.

Likho wailed in pain. The Leshiy dropped the long eyestalks and fell back in terror.

Lebía remembered standing in the middle of the river, seeing Aína lying dead on the other side of the egg. Her Aína. *Her soulbond.*

Then Lebía saw Aína. Or a suggestion of her, more evanescent than smoke—a translucent Sirin of gold that floated up, over her head, growing with strength and intensity like a sunrise in winter.

Lebía felt a brief flare-up of a second heart inside her chest, then it went out.

A final gift, my swan, whispered Aína's voice from some distant land where dead Sirin repose. *The last protection of the hallowed isle of Ghavan.*

Three flames leaped up from the place where the Living Water had flowed. They twined into a serpentine design that dazzled Lebía's vision. The fire smelled sweet, like pomegranates and lavender. The vila, the Leshiy, Likho, and the disembodied head burst into red-gold flame. They screamed in pain and terror. Nothing else burned, as though all the Living Water they had consumed had turned into fire inside them.

Lebía lifted her hand to look at the egg in her palm. Mirnían's face was ashen, his eyes slightly open. His shirt was drenched in the blood pouring from his throat.

The fire continued to twine within itself dizzyingly. Her tears pouring down her face, her chest about to implode from an abyss that seemed to suck at her soul, she fell on her knees before the fire. The fading impression of Aína floated over the fire. She smiled at Lebía, then dissipated.

Lebía dropped the egg into the flames. She didn't know why she did it. It seemed right, somehow.

She fell.

Bright light washed over Lebía's fallen body.

She tried to open her eyes. She couldn't.

CHAPTER 5
CASSÍAN

L ebía lay in place, unwilling to even try to move. In waves, pain like iron claws raked over her body from her neck, down her back, to her legs. But the waves receded until the pain softened to something closer to a caress. Still, her head throbbed. That didn't stop the images from crowding in. Mirnían lying dead in a pool of his own blood. Antomír, his eyes open in surprise, those infernal rose petals still falling. Aína's once-brilliant form darkened by a death that she could have avoided, if not for her involvement with the Ghavanites.

Despair pressed down on Lebía like it hadn't since the dark days after she lost both her parents. She had thought herself capable of happiness, worthy of consolation after a life that she had tried to live well. But all her happiness was lost in a world of illusions, a fabrication of a dark changer. All of her children—it was as though they had never been born. All except Antomír, who was dead. And now Mirnían, who had brought her first darkness to an end with his gentleness and love. He was dead too. She couldn't save him. There was nothing left to live for.

That thought echoed inside her, filling the growing chasms where her heart, her mind used to be.

She blacked out.

❧❧❧

She came back to consciousness fitfully to notice that she was no longer lying down. Nor was the light so bright as to prevent her from opening her eyes. So she did, though even that took an effort of will. She was being carried by a man, she thought, though she could make little of him. He was swathed in furs and leather all the way to his eyes, which were a strikingly dark brown, framed by a sharp set of eyebrows drawn down over his eyes. She thought the eyebrows must have been that serious even when he was a child. They were almost carved into the face, immovable. But the eyes were not wild, nor cruel.

The next thing she remembered was the sensation of falling. No, floating. She cried out instinctively as soon as she awoke. Saying something about being too late, too late. The man—she was sure it was a man now—took her flailing hands firmly, but calmly. Then he did something she never could have expected. He pulled her to himself and began to shush her like a child. He even rocked her.

Lebía became conscious of a loosening inside her. It hurt—that loosening—but the pain was passing. Relief came flooding in with the tears. She passed out again.

Then she was in the light again, and she had no intention of opening her eyes this time. Her hands felt strange. Bulky, as though they weren't hers anymore, but the paws of some kind of animal. Maybe she had become a changer—a punishment for her continued existence while everyone she loved had passed into the land of the dead?

Finally, her eyes opened of their own accord. For a long time, Lebía could do nothing but lie in place, her face toward the ground, as fine details came into focus: a grey pebble with soft brown spots, two ants scurrying between rocks trying to avoid each other at all costs, moss greener than any green ever was.

Her hands were wrapped in rags that were stained brown. Her blood, perhaps? Yes, that's right. She had hurt them badly while running away from the monsters.

"Are you awake, then?" asked a deep voice in the Vasylli tongue, but in a strong accent that she didn't recognize.

She turned her body—she was lying down on a blanket, she realized—to look at the man who had probably saved her life. She found that she could muster no gratitude for that.

"Something like that," she said.

"Ah, you do speak the Mother Tongue," he sounded pleased.

Lebía heard the swish of lazy waves on a seashore made of pebbles. The man's figure, seated before a fire, formed itself in front of her, but he was still nebulous because of the play of sunlight on dappled waves. She had to look down again; it was still too painful.

"You were in a bad state, Soara. I was loath to move you, but that place was such a den of horrors... I hesitate to speak of it before you, Soara. If I had not moved you, I think it would have consumed you."

Why did he call her by that strange name?

"My name is Lebía," she whispered. She could muster no will to say any more.

"Thank you, Soara Lebía," he answered. She could see enough now to notice how he laid his hands on his chest when thanking her. It was a curious, but warm, gesture. "Mine is Cassían. No honorific needed. Indeed, none deserved either." He chuckled, though Lebía sensed, even through the thickness of her own pain, that there was a hint of his own ache in that last sentence. It seemed important. Or it would have to the old Lebía. The one who had always worried about others and lived her life to help them. The Lebía that had died with Mirnían..

She found that she was able to sit up. In that action, she saw that she was also swathed in furs and that the ground around her was covered in a fine powder of snow. She turned away from the man, toward the rippling waves of the lake, or sea, to her right.

As her eyes adjusted to the dancing fire-lights of sun reflected off ripples, she saw a reflection of something far away. A kind of structure, oval in shape. Transparent, or maybe reflecting the surface of the water. Like a very large...

"The egg," said the man, and she turned back to him. "A strange thing, that."

Now his fine details came into focus. His eyebrows were still drawn together and downward as before, but his eyes were gentle, for all that. A patch of dark, shoulder length hair sprouted in a braid from the top of his head, while the area of his temples all the way around his head was shaved completely. Lebía had seen that style of haircut in some very old fresco icons back in Vasyllia. Warrior saints, she remembered. The braid fell on one side of a roughly oval face with strong angles in the cheeks and the line of the nose. He wore a beard, but clearly not for any decoration, only for protection against the cold. No razor of any kind had touched that face for months, she was sure of it.

For a moment, his gaze reminded her of someone. So familiar, and yet... then she realized that if Mirnían had been dark in his coloring, shorter, and stockier in his build, he would look much like this Cassían. That thought did little to dispose him to her, though.

"Do you know what the egg is?" she asked.

"Truly? I do not." He laughed. "I have long wondered at it. But I have rarely braved the approach to it. You have come from there, yes? I had hoped you might tell *me* more about it."

"I must go back," she said, though her body did not react to the urgency in her tone. "My husband..."

"Ah," he said, and there was a hint of wistfulness in that tone. "That is not possible, I'm afraid. There is no entrance to it. Nowhere have I found as much as a chink in that watery armor. How you came out, I know not. As out of a womb, perhaps. A womb that then seals itself shut again." He shook his head in incredulity. "A bad metaphor, I suppose. Forgive me."

He was a strange man. The way he held himself, the way his hands moved, the inflection of his speech—it was so foreign. Yet, he *looked* so Vasylli. She didn't know what to make of it.

"Why did you help me?" she asked, surprised herself at the bitterness in her voice.

He smiled in confusion. "I do not know where you come from, but in the Mother of Cities, where I was born and raised, one does not leave a wounded traveler on the wayside. Especially when all the powers of the darkness seem intent on killing her."

"Even if the traveler wants no help?"

"Especially then, Soara Lebía. For the hurt then is much deeper, and all the more requiring of succor."

"You speak so strangely," she said, unsmiling. She realized, but from a distance, that the old Lebía would not have allowed herself such a rude expression. She didn't care.

She looked back at the egg. The people inside it were still alive, she suspected. All except for Mirnían. It didn't matter: it was her duty to go back and help all the sleepers inside the egg. To bargain with the changer. To explain to him that there was no Living Water. To do...*something*.

Lebía turned away. She had no desire to do any of it. Not anymore.

"And how do you intend to... how did you put it, succor me?" she asked.

He smiled, and for the first time, his eyebrows rose, and she realized he was much younger than she had initially thought. Perhaps thirty, but not even that, she suspected.

"I will let the body tend to itself. The soul I will tend with small, but pleasant, comforts. I live not far from here with my family. There is good ale, warm pies baked this morning, or at least that is what I hope. A hearth-fire. And good conversation, I trust. There is little else, I find, that a weary soul requires for its consolation."

There was a time, perhaps, when she would have agreed with him.

"Where is 'here,' Cassían?" she asked, looking around to see that the shore bordered a line of chalky cliffs topped with scrub brush. Between two of the tallest cliffs was a cleft with a clearly visible road running between them.

"Ah, that is not so easy to answer, Soara Lebía. And I find the comforts of food and drink help much in explicating the mystical."

Lebía laughed for the first time. It was almost as though he were a stage actor reading a play set in the time of Lassar the Blessed. His manner would have been pompous in anyone else. But in him, it was sincere and natural. To her surprise, she realized she did like him.

"I think you may be strong enough to try the first leg of our journey," he suggested tactfully.

She nodded, and he helped her get up on her feet.

CHAPTER 6
A RIFT IN THE REALMS

The road between the cliffs led into the mountain wall through a cave entrance hardly large enough for two to enter side by side. The cliff walls before the cave were so tall that even before walking into it, Lebía was shrouded in darkness. She managed to hobble on her own up to the cleft, but once within, not being able to see the pebbles on the road, she lost her footing more than once, one time even tearing something inside her right ankle so badly that she had to lean on Cassían. He was not much taller than she, but he was strong. It was a different strength than Mirnían's, which was youthful and athletic. Cassían was as though carved from rock. It was a strangely comforting thought.

The cave ended up being more like a tunnel. Even as they entered the mouth, she could see the other end not far ahead. Greenery burst into view, even from a distance. As she approached, she thought she was passing from a realm of shadows into a realm that was the source of all colors. The grass was so green that the name for it was meaningless. The bark of the linden trees clumping near the exit had so many hues, each in distinct shades of brown and grey, that it dizzied her vision.

There weren't many trees, however. It was a totally alien

landscape to her. Towers of stacked rocks stood in rows like trees in a massive forest. The largest of them were thick enough to encompass entire houses, while the thinnest could be encircled by two people holding hands. The rocks came in the strangest variety of hues. From a distance, they looked uniformly grey. But when Lebía came near to one, she noticed splashes of pink and red among the browns and greys. Dark purple fungi grew next to lichens of bright orange. The pillars went on for miles, until they began to coalesce into larger and larger stacks. In the far distance, hazy-blue in the morning light, mountains towered.

Lebía breathed in the air on the other side of the cave as though she hadn't really breathed at all for twenty years. It was so familiar in some way, despite the strangeness of it all. She thought it might be because she, born in a mountain country, had been forced to live on an island for so long. To be back among the giants of rock and earth was like seeing a long-lost grandfather and remembering how he used to hug you and give you secret sweets when you were a child.

"You have not been home for a long time, I think," said Cassían next to her. Lebía realized they had stopped, and she was gaping. She felt herself go red in the face.

"Where do you live, Cassían?" she asked, trying to change the subject.

He pointed toward a clump of the stone pillars, beyond which she saw a plateau covered in grass, leading to an elevated pine forest that stretched as far as the eye could see. Her heart twinged. The forest looked exactly like the forested valley below Vasyllia proper, where Voran used to go hunting for days on end, except viewed as from below, not above.

"You approve." He was smiling, but she thought she detected a hint of amusement at her expense.

She realized she had been smiling. How could she smile? Mirnían was dead. All her children were either dead or... nonexistent.

"Ah, forgive me," he said, and once again, somehow, he was embracing her. She realized that she was sobbing. "You were not ready for my simpleminded levity yet. I am a fool, as you shall see. Come. We will be home soon."

࿔

Lebía forced herself not to look at the countryside. She deserved none of the consolations of this strange place. That she had forgotten Mirnían so quickly only proved how worthless she really was. So she looked at the road. At her feet, clad in boots she hardly recognized, for the last time she remembered wearing them was when she was pregnant with the twins.

The twins who had probably never existed...

Once within the comforting quiet of the forest, she breathed with a little less strain. The carpet of old needles cushioned her steps, and the throbbing pain in her legs lessened. She even began to doze off a little, leaning on Cassían as if he were a trusty pony. He accepted her weight as though she were nothing but a feather.

Lebía smelled woodsmoke before she saw the house. It reposed between two craggy outcroppings that looked out onto a valley with a river running through it. A simple wooden hut with two windows, a door, and beautiful carved storm-shutters flapping slightly in a breeze. The single gable of the hut sported a rough carving of a swan's head. Compared to the wonders of the mansions in Vasyllia's third reach, this place was quaintly rustic. Lebía loved it immediately.

She could not walk up to it, however. Even before they had left the darkest part of the forest, her knees had begun to lock in place as she stepped, forcing her to put all her weight on that strained joint. Each step became like ten stabbing knives.

"Oh, I have pushed you. Forgive me." He picked her up and carried her the rest of the way. In a distant part of where her heart used to be, Lebía felt a flutter. But tiredness came over her, as though being awake was contingent on her feet touching the ground. She was unable to even articulate thanks as he carried her up to the door, which seemed to open of its own accord.

Inside, there was a strange flurry of movement that made her momentarily dizzy. Someone was waving arms and rushing back and forth and trying to tie a head scarf and grab for a ewer of water and a hand towel all at the same time. It was a bit comical, or would have been, had she not vomited onto the ground at that moment, the dizziness pouring out of her with the sickness.

Bundled into something warm, her face wiped with a cool, wet cloth, Lebía felt fire-warmth on her face, fur-softness on her feet, cooling salve on her hands. She sighed and breathed out for what seemed like the first time that day. Had she really been doing nothing but breathing in and holding her breath all day? It certainly felt like it.

"Poor thing, she is... so young." The voice was a woman's, in the same thickly accented Vasylli as Cassían's. Who were these people, anyway?

It was her last coherent thought before she seemed to be absorbed completely into the contemplation of the flickering tongues on the hearth. They were dancing!

ᘓᔓᕄ

Days passed in that fire-edged stupor, accented by warm, spiced ale and hearty food that even Yeda would have enjoyed: mostly pies of various kinds, filled with strong meat like venison and boar. Even the turnips and carrots tasted meaty. The woman refused to let her speak, nor did she allow Cassían to attend to her any longer than a moment or two, when she had to think of her own needs. He stared at her often, but his brows were drawn down again. Not in worry exactly, though the softness at the edge of his eyes was gone now, replaced with something like sorrow, but deeper, more rooted. Something at the level of his marrow.

But she had no strength to think about what it could mean. Who was he? Who was the woman, who seemed older, perhaps old enough to be Cassían's mother, if she had had him very young, though there was an ageless quality about her smooth face. There also seemed to be another person in the hut, but this person never spoke, at least while Lebía was awake. The only thing that gave away his or her existence was the woman's occasional glance in a direction other than Lebía. The woman's entire body position would change when she glanced that way, but Lebía couldn't decipher her expression. She wondered who lay there with her, or if it was some animal: an old cat, perhaps? But as soon as she started wondering about it, she would fall asleep.

Her dreams were mostly calm, except for the occasional appearance of Mirnían. Invariable, he lay gasping on the floor of their bedroom, his hands around his own neck as he tried to stem the flow of blood from his ragged throat. The changer growled loudly in those dreams, but outside her vision. She always woke up in a cold sweat.

"You blame yourself, don't you?" said the woman after one such episode.

Lebía, exhausted by the inexorability of the dreams, turned her face away on her bed, unwilling to talk.

"I will not bore you with any wisdom about there always being two sides to any conflict," pressed the woman, calmly sewing by Lebía's side. "But I will tell you one thing. You should not believe everything you *think* you see in this place."

"Are you suggesting," Lebía leveled her words at the woman with unexpected venom. "That I imagined the death of my beloved?"

"Imagined?" The woman's left eyebrow rose ever so slightly. "Oh no. But perhaps what you saw was in a different time and place, yes? And which time, which place, is the real world?"

Lebía shook her head. Such thoughts, in her state, only thickened the fog in her mind. She turned over and tried to sleep again.

After that conversation, however, Lebía's heart tried to come back to her. Her natural contentment crawled back, as did her love of simple pleasures. Her need to know others and to understand them, so that she could help them in some way—she had grown too used to feeling that way. But as those modes of being tried to return, she turned away from them, guilty. She was not ready to accept a new life, with new pleasures. Not yet. There was still too much to consider, to pour over in her thoughts. What had come about because of her own failures, and what was simple fate? And there was still the strange temptation to drive the sharp pain of her guilt deeper and deeper into the chasm inside her, so that it would become slowly a part of her very nature. There was insidious pleasure in that.

"Your body is much better," said the woman one day.

Lebía was glad she left the rest unsaid, at least in words. Her face was eloquent, though.

"Then it's time to attend to the other," said Cassían from his corner, where he had been reading a book. He put the book down and slapped his palms on his knees, his face all eagerness.

Lebía noticed his right forefinger was black.

"You write as well?" she wondered aloud.

"I do," he said, smiling wryly as he picked up his finger to assess it, as though it were simultaneously a stranger and a familiar friend. "Ah, I see. The quaint rustic poet, says you? No, no. There is good reason for my writing. We will speak of that presently. But your questions first, Soara Lebía."

The woman brought a tray of small pies that smelled of mushrooms and bacon. Next to the pies were two earthen bowls filled with a steaming liquid of some kind, cloudy-brown in appearance. Lebía picked up the bowl first, and the shocking warmth seemed to travel all the way up her arm as she held it. It smelled of nutmeg and clove and milk. Some sort of strong, milky tea. It was delicious.

"Lady," she said, looking at the woman, who today had swathed her head in a headscarf of grey homespun trimmed in a very pleasing ribbon of red and gold. Excellent handiwork. "I am sorry. I have not yet asked your name."

The woman guffawed, her eyebrow arched, as though ironically providing a subtext to her simply-expressed phrase: "No, you have not. My name is Stefania."

Cassían himself started on the cakes, which he devoured, before downing the entire bowl of tea in a single gulp. Lebía felt a bit embarrassed by her small gulps, since she intuited that there was something of the ritual in the way Cassían drank the tea. So she tried to drink the rest also in a single draught. She thought she would choke, or that her throat would burn up from the spicy warmth. Instead, her entire body radiated a pleasant contentment. It was not that far from her daily morning tea in Ghavan...

That thought came on her unexpectedly, as did the faces of her children. She tried to push them away.

"Cassían, tell me please. How is it that you found me near the egg? Coincidence?"

He had leaned back on his armchair, his hands clasped over his wide chest—a picture of domesticity. She almost laughed at it —he looked like an actor pretending to be cozy on stage.

"No, Lebía, not coincidence. I've told you that the egg is normally an object of study for me. There is not much to do here, in this... place. But it is not merely that. Your coming was preceded, as I think I told you, by a concentration of dark powers the like of which I have rarely seen here, even though this place has more obvious manifestations of the Powers than in any other place I have ever lived. You were wanted. I think you still are."

An undercurrent of tension lay behind his words. "Am I putting you in danger?" she asked, but he shook his head and encouraged her to go on.

"What is this place, Cassían? And how did you two come to live here, so far from all other people? Are there even other people here?"

Cassían looked at Stefania—a furtive glance—then nodded to himself. "Permit me to ask you a foolish question, Lebía? What year is it in Vasyllia?"

Lebía felt herself blanch and began to stutter, but Cassían again stopped her with a gesture.

"No, that is unfair. Forgive me. Can you tell me what year it was the last time you saw Vasyllia?"

"Even that's difficult to say.. It was probably near the seventieth year of the second millennium after the Covenant—"

Cassían burst out laughing so raucously that even Stefania, who had shows almost no emotion at all during the days Lebía had been there, seemed perturbed.

"You do my heart a consolation most wondrous," he said, slipping into his formal mode. "Do you not recognize my name, then? Am I to be remembered so badly?"

Lebía's eyes widened and she found that her breathing had gotten lost somewhere between mouth and lungs. "You're... *that* Cassían?"

Cassían the Great, the Dar who began the Golden Age of Vasyllia, who captured the Raven in Vasyllia with the help of the Sirin. The model Dar. Well, now she understood why he looked like Mirnían. Or rather, why Mirnían looked like him. What a tremendous thing, for that likeness to last for more than five hundred years!

"Please, Soara Lebía," he said, subsiding a little, and revealing that his laughter was at least partially hysterical by the red spots on his cheeks and the widened whites of his eyes. "I beg that you say nothing of your knowledge of my reign. I will tell you as much as I can, but you must not let me know anything of what *may* transpire in my future."

What in the Heights does that mean? Her shoulders tensed slightly.

"Have you heard of what I did to my beloved princess?"

"The story of the eagle and the swan," Lebía said. "That actually *happened?*"

The story, which had not made it into any of the *Old Tales*, had been dramatically reintroduced to Vasyllian ears by the Pilgrim in the first days of the fall of Vasyllia, what seemed so many years ago now. He had told of how Cassían had encountered the Raven in the wild. Enticed by his false promises, Cassían had allowed himself to be transformed into an eagle. While in a state of rapture as the king of the skies, he had allowed his animal nature to possess him. In a fit of bestial rage, he had killed a swan. A black swan. It turned out she had been his own beloved princess, also transformed by the power of the Raven.

Cassían lowered his face to look at his hands, now cupped on his knees before him. His relaxed composure had gone completely. He was tense as a drum-head.

"It did. Somehow, with the good grace of the Heights, the Sirin found me after I had committed that vile act. They even helped me capture the Raven, that foulness that had seduced me. You must know that he was imprisoned for a time in Vasyllia."

Lebía nodded.

"Yes, well, then you must also know how he escaped, and at the hand of my own daughter. Perhaps you know, Soara, that children are put on this earth to enact all of their parents' failings in the worst possible way, yes?"

Lebía smiled into her tea.

"Thank you for your sympathy," he said, half sarcastically. "I could not rest after he escaped. How much calamity can I unleash on my own people, I asked myself? Then the reports rushing in—plague in Karila, blight on Nebesta's crops, strange madness in both speechless creatures and men. To top it all, reports of the Raven coming close to finding Living Water... But I see by your eyes that you know all this..."

"More than that..." she said. "It is happening again in my time."

At that, he was struck dumb for a full minute. She realized

she may have said something that was not merely careless, but that could impact her own future. The thought was a difficult one to consider, and yet, after the egg and its parallel reality, anything was possible.

"Highness," she said without thinking, "I will not say much, except to tell you that what you do in your life ensures prosperity until the days of my generation."

He seemed to remember that it was necessary to breathe in order to continue living.

"You confirm the dearest hope of my heart. It is the reason I write in this book, which will be the record of my thoughts for my heirs alone. A secret apocrypha for those who need to know."

A dark shadow seemed to pass over his face. He shook his head, slightly.

"No, I must be wary of what I say henceforth," he said, continuing in a subdued tone. "But you are here with me, so you must know some of what has happened. This place where we live. It is not Vasyllia... or rather, not *yet* Vasyllia."

A feathery touch of understanding teased her, but fled like mist. He leaned back again and closed his eyes as he crossed his arms over his chest.

"There was a dendrite near Vasyllia in my time. A man living on top of a tree, where he contemplated the mysteries of the Heights. A very strange man, perhaps even mad. But he had the power of prophecy. True prophecy, not the kind that panders for the sake of money. He told me that it was my responsibility that the Raven had escaped, and that the future of Vasyllia depended on my catching him. He also gave me something of inestimable worth. A way of passing into the Mids of Aer, where it was said the Raven was hiding and searching for Living Water.

"I reached the Mids of Aer through some rather strange roads. It's a story unto itself. Perhaps for another time. But I took a wrong turn. If you've ever been in any of the other Realms, you'll know they are perilous places that follow no logical ordinances. We who are of the earth have no right to expect them to have such things. And then, I fell."

He wouldn't say how that happened, and she didn't press him.

"Literally, in fact. From the Mids to a different place entirely. This place. I found myself in the forest that we crossed when you arrived. Stefania was kind enough to take me in. She and dear Derzhava. Stefania had also come here by accident. But she has yet to tell me how."

"And nor will I, Cassían, till I think it right," she said from a corner, knitting and looking down at a bundle of clothes next to her. Lebía realized that it wasn't a bundle of clothes. It was a person.

"Come," said Stefania, reaching a hand to Lebía. "Meet our other overgrown baby."

"Someday," said a completely new voice Lebía hadn't heard yet. "You'll come up with a better joke, Stefania."

Lebía got up. At first, it felt like her bones had grown into her skin, and her muscles had turned to wood. She hadn't gotten up from her pallet near the hearth for days, she remembered. But after about a hundred clicking joints and creaking muscles she didn't realize she had, she limped over to the bench by the window where Stefania sat knitting. Next to her lay a girl. Or her face looked like a girl's of about twelve. But her body looked more like a tree branch wrapped in fabric. She had no hands— her arms ended in misshapen stumps. Lebía saw no feet under the blankets, but the girl's legs were too short to have feet. And her torso, as much as she could tell, was a lumpy mass of misshapen flesh and bone.

"Quite a sight, I know," said Derzhava, looking at Lebía. "You'll grow used to it."

"How old are you, child?" asked Lebía.

"I'm twenty seven," Derzhava answered, her twisted smile a ray of light on a face as twisted as her back.

"They found me," said Cassían, "and they helped heal me. So

I have given my life to their care and protection. There is no way out of this land, as far as I can tell. There are... barriers all around. Like the eggshell of the place you inhabited. I have yet to find any doorway out."

"But what is this place, then?" persisted Lebía. "Is it a different Realm of Aer?"

"When I was traveling the Mids, something happened," he answered, "Something cataclysmic, I think. Not in my time. Perhaps in yours. A rift opened between the Realms. Bits and pieces of all times and places fell into it before the rift closed in on itself. This is a place outside the Realms. Or between them, perhaps. This bit of mountainous land is Vasyllia before there were men on it. Before there was even a Mount Vasyllia. It is ancient beyond all reckoning. But safe it is not. Some dark Powers were trapped here when the rift closed."

"Wait," said Lebía, confused. "How can you be sure? Or are you guessing?"

He smiled warily. "Come," he said. "It's time you saw."

CHAPTER 7
THE STONE OF ALATYR

Behind the house, on a narrow plain between the two crags, stood two pens filled with pigs. Goats roamed outside the pens—at least ten of them. A single plow horse grazed in the distance lazily. The rest of the land, all the way to a cliff edge about a bow shot away, was plowed and planted with various grains, vegetables, and fruit trees. Lebía laughed at the sight.

"I thought you had said that there wasn't much to do in these parts?" she said turning to Cassían.

He had thrown on a light cape and hood with no fur lining it. It was only then that Lebía realized that it was balmy, warm even. But hadn't there been snow on the shore where she had woken up?

"Yes," he answered, when she asked. "There was snow there. But this is a different part of the Rift-realm. You didn't feel it when you passed through the cleft in shoreline cliffs?"

She had, only she had been too tired to think it was anything other than her fancy.

"I was only jesting a little when I said that, Lebía," Cassían continued. "About there being nothing to do here. This is the closest to a primeval paradise that exists, I believe. In fact, it may be *the* primeval paradise. The ground... well, fruitful says nothing. All I have to do is clear the ground, put a seed in, then forget about it. I don't even have to water it. And there are no tares, no weeds of any kind. The pigs? They forage on their own. The goats, though wild, never leave, and present themselves to be milked by Stefania. It is the strangest thing you will ever see."

"What sort of luck put you here, Cassían, instead of in the dying Vasyllia of my time?" She had tried to pass it off as a joke, but as soon as she said it, she realized that it wasn't, not at all.

His stormy face was a marked contrast to the idyll before her —setting sun shining on brilliant-green grass, the goats' fur almost gilded by the light.

"Come," he said, and led her toward the cliff edge. As they approached, Lebía saw that the crags on the right were shorter than the cliff side on the left. Near an edge that plunged hundreds of feet down to a rolling valley with four rivers inter-lacing through grassland and wild groves of some kind of fruit-bearing trees, a road appeared at the far end of the right crag. It became a set of rough stairs that hugged the edge of the cliff. It was too near the drop for Lebía's tastes, but when Cassían led her toward it, she followed.

"Tell me, Lebía," he said, turning his head so she, walking behind him now, could hear. "Tell me of the horrors of your time."

She did.

As she did, his shoulders seemed to rise and come closer together, until he looked more vulture than man. The tension practically stank on him. After she had finished, she realized there was absolutely nothing but a sheer drop to her left, begin-ning no more than a yard to the left of the stairs, which still went up gradually. With a pang of gratitude, she realized he had been trying to distract her at the cost of his own self-possession.

"I see it is perhaps even worse for you than it was for me," he said, after she fell silent. "You can understand my pain then. You can understand when I tell you that I do not sleep at night often, because I see the faces—individual faces—of the hundreds of people who came to the walls of Vasyllia from the Outer Lands covered in sores, their bodies black from the plague, their minds addled from the pain. You can understand when I tell you that children were dying by the hundreds within Vasyllia herself, because all the crops failed three years running. And here I sit in paradise and plough perfect ground, eating cakes baked by a goddess of the hearth."

Yes, Lebía understood. He had stopped, apparently too full of remembrance to go on for a moment. Before she knew what she was doing, she had placed her left hand on his shoulder. His shoulders tensed for a moment at that touch, then relaxed. The vulture became a man again.

"I have done all I can to try to find the way out," he said, taking her arm in his—a familiar gesture, even a brotherly one. Or, she thought wryly, the gesture of a great-great-great-grandfather to his great-great-great-grandson's wife. "Now, all I have left is an offering to the lord of this place. It is my hope that he sees my love for Stefania, my care for Derzhava. Perhaps he will be moved."

He wasn't speaking metaphorically, she realized.

"Look," he said, moving just enough for her to come up to the step above him on the cliff-wall side, not the precipice side.

Lebía gasped.

"What... in all the ..."

She looked up at a small clearing of rock just ahead of them —a circular, shallow bowl, cleared of anything but smooth stone. Too smooth to be natural. At the point of the bowl nearest the cliff edge stood a boulder, roughly weathered into the shape of a table. It faced a massive sculpture of white stone—a stag with antlers impossibly large. The stag was three times the size of any deer she had ever seen, except perhaps the white stag. It was a sight that wasn't simply improbable. Simply put, it should not exist. Not in a place with no human beings. It had been carved by a masterful hand that left no fine detail of the stag to chance. If someone had told her that this was a real beast that had been turned to stone, she would have believed it.

"It is an altar. Possibly the first altar ever built in Vasyllia-to-be. I come here every morning to offer my supplication."

"An altar," she repeated. "To whom?"

"You'll see," he said. "If we are blessed, tomorrow."

⚜

They returned every morning for a week, but nothing happened. Lebía began to think that perhaps Cassían, broken by his failures as a Dar and his captivity in paradise, had lost his mind and was seeing visions. But that didn't prevent his growing in her estimation by the day.

It was his treatment of Derzhava that shocked her. Vasyllia was a land of warriors, a land of hard men, some of whom would only show gentleness in private, to their wives and children. But hardly any warrior ever showed affection and care for someone like Derzhava. There were places where children born with such ailments were taken. Places run by clerics and nurses. Not very nice places.

But Cassían began every morning, after their return from the altar, by washing Derzhava completely from head to foot—so to speak— with his own hands. After the first day, when Lebía had struggled with revulsion so thick it made her want to vomit, Lebía helped him. If she thought it was an easy task, she was quickly disabused of that notion. Derzhava was covered in festering sores. Only a thorough washing, followed by an anointing with a special salve made by Stefania, prevented the rot from becoming pervasive, and in some cases some sores were actually healed. The smell was unbearable. Lebía had once been in a slaughterhouse in Vasyllia. She had had to work at cleaning a public latrine in childhood as a punishment. Those smells were roses and lilac blooms compared to Derzhava's sores.

Cassían genuinely did not notice the smell, and he treated Derzhava's twisted, broken body like it was a relic or a jewel. She never spoke when he washed her, only looked at him with eyes that were too wide for her face. The expression was hard to read for Lebía, and when Derzhava turned to look at her, she couldn't hold her gaze for longer than a second. There were emotions behind those eyes that Lebía had never even imagined, much less felt, even in the worst of days.

Then he would carry Derzhava outside, where she would spend her day looking out at the idyllic pastoral before her. He did some small work on the fields. Lebía helped with pleasure, the work reminding her of the early years on Ghavan, when she had worked the land with the rest of the villagers too. Then, he would tell Derzhava stories of Old Vasyllia. Lebía listened with pleasure, learning a great deal about her home that she had never known. Much had been lost in the five hundred years separating them.

About a week later, Lebía and Cassían were both outside, harvesting tomatoes that were riper, larger, and redder than any Lebía had tasted in her life. She had wandered a way off from Cassían, lost in the velvety smell of tomatoes and earth. The smell reminded her of a day, early in her married life, when Mirnían had surprised her one morning by bringing a platter of fresh tomatoes and cheese to their bed. It was possibly the only morning in their married life when Mirnían had woken up before she had. She hadn't understood why, until he reminded her that it was ten years to the day after she healed him from leprosy.

She realized she had only thought of Mirnían once during the past weeks. Her hopeless boy. The only person who knew exactly which spot behind her right ear thrilled her the most. All worries, all troubles—he made everything better. Even when he was the one at fault. And she had failed to save him.

Her chin shuddered uncontrollably. What was happening to

her? A stabbing pain jabbed the back of her neck. She tried to swallow, but it was like she had eaten cotton fibers for breakfast.

There was a stone lying on the bed of tomatoes. Sharp on one edge. Perfect for slicing her wrist. Perfect for the only punishment she deserved.

She reached for the stone.

"Do you know why I'm alive?" Derzhava said. Lebía hadn't realized she had strayed so close to the house. She dropped the stone as though it were a heated iron pot. Her hands shook. It took her three tries to fix the hair that had fallen over her face.

"What do you mean, Derzhava?" she asked, her voice still shaky.

"Because I refuse to die," she said. "This body... it should have killed me twenty years ago. My will fights it. Every moment of every day."

"But why, Derzhava?" asked Lebía, sitting next to her.

"Are you so blind? To the world outside and inside?" She pointed with her chin. The sun had just cleared a bank of clouds, pregnant with rain. As it did, a rainbow encircled the sun like a halo of many-colored flames. The tension that had gripped Lebía faded into nothing. Her entire body seemed to fade with the tension, until she was almost floating. She realized she had a stupid grin on her face.

With a start, she turned to Derzhava.

"Did you do that? How?"

Derzhava laughed. "I didn't do anything. But people do tend to get a sense of... perspective when they're around me. It gives me joy, you know." She looked, with her rosy cheeks and lop-sided smile, like she had slept for weeks on end. How was she able to find so much joy with so little to work with?

"Don't let her humility fool you," said Stefania, suddenly appearing at Lebía's elbow with a basket under her arm. "Derzhava is a seer. A gift to leaven her suffering, I suppose."

Derzhava actually blushed as Stefania walked away into the

garden. Lebía, unexpectedly embarrassed, turned to see Cassían looking at her. He was in his linen work shirt, open at the throat. He hadn't bothered to braid his hair today, and it fell around his shaved temples in a pleasing disarray. The sun caught the dark brown of his eyes, and they shone with a slightly green tinge. She hadn't seen that color in his eyes before. It was different from Mirnían's ice-blue, but in every other way, he looked so much like Mirnían that her breath caught in her chest.

She missed him so much. But for the first time, there was an afterglow of sweetness to the remembrance.

"He is a good man. Take it from me," said Derzhava, a light in her eyes. "And he admires you, you know."

"Me? Whatever for?" Lebía looked down, the shard of guilt in her heart reminding her of its existence with a painful stab. "I have done nothing here. Only taken from you all."

"You don't see it, do you? You killed his darkness dead, a while back."

He smiled at them, then turned back to his work. Yes, Lebía did see a change. He was no longer carrying a cloud behind him like a leashed horse. A quiet hope had come back to him.

Could she ever learn to hope again?

꧁꧂

That afternoon she spent with Stefania in the small back room of the house that served as both food pantry and kitchen. They chopped more carrots than they would need for a month, but Stefania never complained, as though she understood that Lebía needed repetitive motions to distract herself from herself. She said nothing the entire time, though Lebía felt her gaze on her constantly. She refused to look at her.

As the afternoon faded to evening, the tension inside Lebía seemed to spread itself out into the air of the house. Even Derzhava, when Lebía stole a look at her lying on her bench in the hearth-room, staring at the sky as each new star was born, seemed emptied of her previous joy.

With a pang in her chest, Lebía wondered if she would ever again find a place or a time when she could be calm and at peace.

A light flashed outside—lightning out of a clear sky. The hut shook as though some wyrm of the underground had come up from under its foundation and was now trying to push the house up out of the ground. Stefania, her jaw set, looked out the window. She must have seen something truly apocalyptic for her usual imperturbable self to blossom into a smile like the sun rising. At Lebía's wide eyed gaze, she grudgingly answered.

"Something unexpected, my dear. And very, very promising." She looked Lebía deeply into her eyes. "I think you're about to be tested, swanling." Lebía almost jumped at that diminutive. It had been Voran's favorite for her. "Poor Cassían. Here he comes, at the bidding of the high and mighty one he puts so much hope in." Her voice dripped with scorn.

"So there is some sort of Power at work here? I had assumed Cassían's belief to be false."

"Oh, he's real enough, that *Power*," Stefania said, her voice frosty. "But before you assume that this Power will come swooping down to save you all, think of this, my girl. What sort of a High Being would rule a place that keeps its denizens imprisoned in various realms of perfect contentment, with no discernible way out? Think of your artisan, for one. I'm sure he was dripping with virtue from head to toe."

Lebía's heart raced. "Wait, you know about Ghavan? How?"

Stefania came up to Lebía and took both her hands. They were large, strong hands. Motherly hands.

"You are a wise woman, Lebía, even in this Realm of illusions. Whatever you think you know about the world of the egg, trust your inner light. Your soul-bond with Aína may be shattered, yes. But no one touched by the Sirin can fail to have that love, that wisdom live on inside her. Trust it. It is the strongest gift you have from the Unknown Father."

Lebía's heart skipped a beat, though she didn't exactly understand. *What Unknown Father is this?*

Cassían, already dressed for the walk, poked his head into the kitchen.

"Will you come?" he asked Lebía.

She nodded.

CHAPTER 8
THE GOD APPEARS

The clearing before the altar was pitch black when they came to it, then, as they entered, ghostly and barely illumined by the light of Cassían's lantern. But something above the antlers of the great stag roiled in the darkness, as though clouds darker than the sky were spinning a storm into existence. No wind came from that blackness, but the sounds of the worst storm she had ever heard pummeled her head. She tried to shut her ears with her hands, but the sound was as though inside her already.

The skies tore apart, and the light streaming from the rent was almost liquid. To her surprise, she realized she could look into it. There was a face in the midst of the light—a warrior whose face was the sun, whose hair was the sun's aureole, whose eyes were the stars. He wore a helm of red-gold, from the peak of which fire sprouted like a fountain. His breastplate was a snarling lion of bronze. He had a spear tipped with fire in his left hand. His right was extended toward Cassían, who was on his knees before this lord of the skies. She did the same, almost without thinking

"Is that who I think it is?" She hissed in his ear. Her beating heart sounded louder in her ears than her own words. Like all good Vasylli, she was a faithful adherent of the cult of Adonais. But she preferred her divinities distant and kindly. This was not the Adonais she expected.

Cassían smiled at her, then took her hand in his. "Yes. Adonais himself."

Lebía chuckled nervously. She felt Cassían's adoration spill over into her own heart.

What a thing in my life, to be a soul-bond to a Sirin, then to actually see Adonais!

The light around the god flared so brightly, they had to bow their heads down to the ground. Then the light disappeared, and all was darkness again. For a moment, Lebía was sure that she had been blinded.

"Stand up, my children," said a kind voice, deeper than any human voice ever was. It was immediately to their right.

Lebía jumped up and faced the man who stood before them. A bearded man, hair peppered with grey and white, dressed in a luxurious red robe that even a king would only wear at the most important occasions. He gave off a soft light—the only indication that he wasn't human.

Cassían fell at his feet and kissed the gold-embroidered hem of his robes. The god smiled down at him and patted his head.

"My loyal one," he said. "I have kept myself from you for so long, only seeing you from afar for so long! I know you have asked for me to come. There was no time. And now there is even less time."

"Lord, I have brought a faithful daughter of yours from Vasyllia," said Cassían.

"Yes, Lebía the daughter of Otchigen. I have watched you for a long time. Your coming has long been foretold. And you have set off events that will shake the foundation of the times, as well as the worlds."

Lebía fell on her knees again. Her heart was so full of love, she thought it would burst. She wanted to run to Adonais, to hug his feet, to cry on his shoulder. This was exactly the kind of fatherly figure she could spill all her wounded heart to.

But Stefania's words kept popping into her head annoyingly. Why on earth had she warned her to be on her guard? This was Adonais himself!

"My son, my daughter," said the god. "I wish we could rest here together and speak of the great mysteries of the Heights. Of the end of all times. But that time will yet come, Cassían. First, I come to grant your supplication. For your long tending of my daughter Derzhava, I will restore you to the Vasyllia of your time. I will renew covenant between your people and the Heights, and a Golden Age of Vasyllia will begin."

Lebía's heart soared, then plunged again. What else could Adonais have for her, save for eternal punishment for her failing her people?

"But even your virtue is only the first step, Cassían. You must prove your faith in me."

"Anything, Lord. I will do anything for you."

"Yes, I don't doubt you, my son. You must bring me a sacrifice here, at this most ancient of my altars, the Stone of Alatyr. You must offer me the life of the one you hold dearest in the world. I ask you to give me Derzhava's life."

Lebía gasped audibly. Cassían began to shake visibly as he took his face in his own hands.

"I feel your hurt, my son. But do not fret. It need not be painful, my child. You know Derzhava has suffered too long. It will be a mercy. Stefania has a bottle of strong soporific in the pantry. Give Derzhava a draught of it. I will cover her pain forever, and she will be at peace. Then bring her here. The pyre is already placed."

He pointed, and now Lebía saw that a wood pyre had been placed on the Stone of Alatyr.

"Lord," Cassían began.

"However," Adonais's voice boomed over Cassían's soft rejoinder. "You must hurry. Look!"

He pointed over the edge of the cliff down to the valley below. Between two forests, something dark heaved and writhed. It looked like a huge snake. At the head of the snake were seven lights, like the eyes of a spider. Lebía couldn't see more, but her imagination provided more than enough detail. A monster from the nether regions of this in-between place, no doubt.

"You saw the flash of light, felt the earthquake, did you not, my children? That was the coming of this abomination from the Abyss. It is destroying all of this Realm in its passing. I will close the final gate on it, and it will perish in its own fires. In the fires that will consume this Nether-realm forever. You will come with me. You will all come with me to my country first, then to your proper places in the times of Vasyllia. But first, you must prove yourselves loyal of my trust. For the trials that await all of you still are great. You must steel yourselves for them with my power. A power I give to my faithful. The ones who prove their faith in me."

⚕

Only after they were halfway down the stairs did Lebía begin to doubt.

Why does Adonais demand the death of an innocent woman?

She tried to laugh off the thought as silly. He was the Creator; he could do as he wished. And he offered them the ultimate gift. Of course the gift would cost much.

But what about Derzhava? Does she deserve to die?

No.

After all, there was only one person in this realm who no longer served any purpose. Only one expendable person.

Lebía stopped dead in her tracks, so suddenly, that she almost slipped down the stairs. The scrabbling noise of her feet made Cassían stop and turn around.

"What is it, Lebía?"

Lebía's knees buckled. It didn't matter that she had made the decision; she was still afraid. But this was the only right thing to do. And what sort of a daughter of Otchigen was she? She would see them all again soon, so soon. What right had she to be afraid?

"Cassían, have I done some good here, in these few days? Or have I truly only been a burden to you all?"

His eyes shone through his smile. In a man of his strength and bearing, it was strangely affecting. "I beg your forgiveness, Lebía. I didn't tell you. I thought everyone could see. Your coming lifted a darkness from my shoulders that I had despaired of ever casting off. Your presence, and the presence of a new Vasyllia through you—I can now do what I must. I can make this sacrifice and win the second covenant with Adonais."

"That is good. For it will be harder than you know."

He looked up at her sharply, his eyes uncomprehending. Then they widened, and his stony eyebrows rose so high, she was afraid they would split his head open.

"Lebía, you're not suggesting...."

"It is necessary, Cassían. I have lived a full life, I see it behind me like a tapestry so long and ornate that the other end is invisible. And I will do one final thing before I rest. I will return Vasyllia her golden Dar."

He embraced her with all the fiery strength typical of Otchigen, whose bear-embraces she could still remember from distant childhood. Given their precarious perch, this could have been fatal for both of them. But he was like a stone. A stone that was weeping hot tears on her shoulder.

"You are right," he said. "You are the dearest thing to me in this place. It is silly, I suppose, but you are, in some strange way, a daughter of mine."

Lebía chuckled at the thought. He was, of course, a distant, ancient ancestor of her husband, but in appearance he was the same age as she, if not younger.

"Lebía, I have come to value your company, your keen mind

and gentle heart. Your loss will gouge my heart. It is fitting that *you* be sacrifice. But how... how can I do it?"

"I will help you, my Dar," she said, disentangling herself from his embrace and falling before him onto her knees. He took her hands and lifted her—a regal gesture of a lord accepting a great gift from his retainer.

Lebía sighed, and felt joy for the first time in weeks.

CHAPTER 9

SACRIFICE

Adonais stood beside the Stone of Alatyr, holding a lit torch in his hand. His eyes looked at them kindly, but changed when he saw they were alone.

"Have you then failed me, my children?" he said, the tears evident in his voice. A wave of sorrow rose inside Lebía, almost as though imposed from outside herself.

Cassían fell on his knees before Adonais and extended his arms outward in the pose of the supplicating slave.

"No, Great Lord. You have told me that I must sacrifice the one who is dearest in my heart. That is no longer Derzhava. It is Lebía of Vasyllia."

A strange expression flitted over the face of Adonais. There was something strange about the shifting of that expression. *Why does he suddenly look so familiar?*

Adonais smiled. "The daughter of the one who stood up to the Raven and defeated him, even after possession? It is a worthy gift to seal Covenant. My daughter, do you do this willingly?"

She had to breathe twice to get the necessary air in her lungs. "I do, Lord."

Her heart clenched in fear. Adonais's eyes. They had flared in fire. They were... hungry. This was not... it could not be...

"So be it," he said, allowing the first "S" to linger sibilantly. Her limbs were frozen in place. She had no control over them. She began to move toward the pyre unwillingly. Cassían wasn't looking at her. He was taking the fire from Adonais's hands. She climbed up awkwardly, as though someone else were pushing her limbs for her and didn't yet know how to handle them properly. Something slithered inside her head, and she heard a voice.

"How fitting, my dear. You failed with the Living Water, but this way is far better."

Lebía's heart stopped beating for a moment as she recognized the voice. It was the artisan. Not Adonais at all.

She forced herself to think the words at him: "You dare take up the form of Adonais? You think he cannot see you, even in this forgotten realm?"

The artisan's voice chuckled in her head, though the form of Adonais continued to stare at her hungrily. Cassián was moving slowly toward her with the torch.

"Ha! You fool. There is no Adonais. Adonais is only a face of the Raven. And this *sacrifice?* Complex blood magic. Your blood, mixed with earth power and fire, and I *think* I can open a portal out of this place finally. Living Water would have made it easier, you know."

He sounded genuinely affronted, as though she were responsible for a great deal of trouble.

"What about your egg, the world inside it?" *What about my family?*

"What do I care? They were meant to serve a purpose but you all failed. Don't you feel at all comforted that despite your failure, you're still instrumental to all this? To the greatest deception ever perpetrated on the proud nation of Vasyllia."

The face of Adonais shifted, its eyes comprehending some new, unexpected truth.

"They'll call *me* the new Harbinger. Oh, the feasting I'll have on Vasyllia's blood! A glorious age for the Mother of Cities, founded on a false covenant!"

"What are you talking about?"

"You really are a thick-headed race. You and Cassían have made an agreement as representative of Vasyllia, sealed in blood, in the name of Adonais. It is the forging of a new covenant. The Raven will accept this as a gift from me and raise me higher than any of my brothers."

An icy hand seemed to squeeze her heart, preventing her from breathing. Cassían was looking at her, holding the torch in his hand. Tears fell down his face freely. He was saying something, but something seemed to block her hearing.

She pushed with all her might against the invisible bonds holding her in place. She screamed in her mind at Cassían: *Look at me! Look at me! Don't do this!*

He stared right at her, but saw nothing of what was passing through her head.

He lit the pyre.

The fires jumped as though they had been waiting for years to consume her. The hem of her dress caught fire. The smell was sharp and rank. The smell of burning hair was next.

Goodbye, Lebía. I did enjoy living in your company all those years. You have a lovely family.

The smoke burned her eyes, but she kept them open. She saw, in silhouette, how Adonais took Cassían by the hand. Adonais's face took on an intense concentration. Sweat beaded on his forehead. Pain consumed Lebía. She screamed.

A rent in the fabric of the world appeared before Adonais and Cassían. They both flashed in bright light, then were gone.

It was done. She had failed, even more terribly than she could ever have imagined.

"Don't be so maudlin," said Stefania's voice next to her. It was different now, strong like tempered steel. Stefania was now a figure wreathed in fire next to her on the Stone of Alatyr. "Ah, but I forget. You're just Vasylli." It was said with the kind of sarcasm a mother reserves for the silliness of her favorite daughter.

"What are you, Stefania?" asked Lebía, realizing that it was her own mouth that moved, her own voice that spoke. And she could move her limbs, as much as that made any difference. She was already more than half-burned, she realized. It now hurt a lot less than before.

"As human as you, my dear. And a sister of the fire, so to speak." She sounded pleased at the sound of that phrase. "My real name is Alienne Dolgoruk of the Nebesti."

Alienne embraced her, and Lebía smelled tuberose and orange. The embrace was like motherhood distilled to a touch.

Lebía's last thought was of Zabían and how he stuck out his tongue as he held that blasted banner in place. She laughed, the tears sizzling on her face. Then, she died.

CHAPTER 10
A NEW WORLD

"**S**leeping beauty," said Mirnían in a half-whisper, a laugh suppressed just beneath it. "Breakfast."

Lebía awoke with the stench of smoke still in her nostrils. She jerked in place so violently that Mirnían dropped the tray he held in his hands. Tea, cakes, and tomatoes now made a new decoration on their bedroom floor. Mirnían stared at the mess with wide eyes, then dissolved into a hearty laugh.

So this was what the land of dead was like, she thought with a chuckle. Remarkably similar to her own life.

"I'm sorry, love. I should have known that you'd still be jumpy after yesterday."

Something was very, very wrong about this land of the dead. It looked no different from Ghavan.

"Yesterday?" she felt as stupid as a newborn child. *What in all the blessed Heights is going on?*

"When they fitted the rose window in the temple. You started screaming. Ran out of the church, then fell into some sort of a stupor. You've been sleeping it off since. You don't remember?"

"Remember? What...?" she choked on her own saliva and started to cough.

Adelaida burst into the room, only stopping for a moment to assess the damage. She shook her head, seemed to decide it wasn't important, and continued with her message:

"You need to see this, Mama, Papa. There's... well... a white stag..."

Lebía's heart jumped almost as high as she did out of the bed.

☙☙☙

All of Ghavan had come to see it.

A white stag stood at the shore of the Great Sea, beyond the place where there should have been a transparent eggshell dividing Ghavan from the rest of the Realms. It was no longer there. Stefania, or rather Alienne, Lebía remembered, held Derzhava in her arms as she sat mounted on the white stag, the same one who had guided Lebía to Ghavan in the first place, so many years ago. He looked exactly like the stone buck at the Stone of Alatyr.

"Rejoice, Lebía!" said Alienne. "Your sacrifice has been found acceptable before the throne of the Most High, the Unknown Father. Your death gave life to the white stag at the beginning of all times in Vasyllia. You have set in place the events that will save Vasyllia from its own fall."

Then Alienne... changed. But not like a changer. Her face became younger, her hair darkened into a color like black opal, and a pair of fiery wings adorned her shoulders.

"Don't look at me like that," said Alienne, and Stefania's annoyed imperiousness had come back in droves. "I'm still human, you know. Just... *more* human than before. Transfiguration. A gift given after the seventh baptism of fire."

Lebía silently expelled her breath in utter awe. These were mysteries that even the *Sayings* only mentioned obliquely.

Mirnían approached the white stag and fell before it on his knees. It lowered its head and touched his head with its nose. He breathed deeply, as though refreshed, and stood up to face Alienne.

"But," Lebía couldn't understand what was happening. "If I died... is this... the land of the dead?"

"No, my dear," said Derzhava, looking radiant in the arms of Alienne. "You died, but by your death you have broken the walls of the egg. You've destroyed the power of the artisan in this place. And the Unknown Father has given you a great gift. He returned your soul to your body in the moment just after you saw the vision in the temple. And he has given life to all your children. You have made New Ghavan possible."

Lebía turned around, and there they were. Adelaida, her seriousness on the verge of tearful collapse. Kachinka and Marinka embracing each other's waist, already crying. Zabían sticking his ridiculous tongue out, trying to understand what was happening. They were real. They were alive.

All of them, seeing her face, ran to her. She embraced them all, her shaking body matching the heaving of her chest as she sobbed into Marinka and Kachinka's hair. They smelled of nutmeg and cloves. Strong arms embraced her from the back. She turned around and kissed him. That taste—she thought she would never again experience its headiness. It almost broke her heart in two. She melted into his embrace.

"Look!" cried a child in the crowd.

An awed murmur came over everyone, followed by reverent silence.

Lebía turned around. Seven longboats with carved swans at the prows approached Ghavan from afar. As they approached, Lebía saw that each boat had a single aged warrior with long white hair and beard standing in it, holding a banner aloft. Each banner bore a silver tree with white blossoms, with three streams of blue water pouring from the roots. The banner of old Vasyllia from the time of Cassían the Great. Lebía laughed from sheer exhilaration.

Behind the seven boats was an armada of smaller boats, filled to brim with warriors bristling with spears. The banners that rose from the boats were strange—little more than brown rags.

"By my..." said Mirnían, breathless. "Those are Gumiren spirit-banners. I don't understand. How can old Vasylli banners go together with Gumiren spirit-banners. Should I call the warriors to my aid?"

"No, my love," said Lebía, putting her hand on his cheek. He leaned into it, then kissed her palm. Charges like lightning jumped up and down her spine. "Let me handle this, please."

He nodded, smiling wryly. "Could I ever deny you anything, my love?"

CHAPTER 11
HISTORY REWRITTEN

The room in Ghavan's central inn was more than usually warm. All the tables had been removed save for a single, long trestle. The hearth-fire blazed, and two piglets roasted on it, wrapped with bacon and with an apple in each mouth. The smell of candles and roast meat filled the space. Tankards of ale foamed before each person sitting at the table. But that was where the coziness ended.

Lebía could cut the tension in the room with Mirnían's sword, and it would hardly give. She sat at the head as the hostess, and across from her sat Alienne of the Nebesti in her transfigured form, save for the wings of fire. Alienne had just explained to them all who she was in her previous life. To her right sat two Gumiren—they gave their names as Etchigu and Batuk. She liked Etchigu's open expression and lively eyes. Batuk looked like Lebía had herself probably looked during the darkest moment before her first death.

Or whatever it was that had happened to her.

Mirnían sat across from the Gumiren, his expression guarded. That expression actually gave her hope. It was what he looked like when he intended to be fair-minded, no matter what his natural inclination. She knew she had helped forge that expression after many years of life on Ghavan. Years that had all been real, in spite of the artisan's lies.

"There's one thing I don't understand," Mirnían was saying as Lebía returned from her reverie to the ongoing conversation. Batuk was pouring the ale. He already looked the better for having drunk an entire tankard. Etchigu was chuckling as he looked at him. "Lebía explained that there were two realities, two nested worlds. One was Ghavan, the other a vision of primeval Vasyllia. So which is real?"

"Neither is real," said Derzhava, who lay near them at the hearth. Lebía had been pleased to see that the Gumiren showed her a special deference. "Not *truly* real. When the Sirin pushed Ghavan out of the Lows of Aer after Antomír broke the taboo and killed the covenant tree, they could not complete the push to the Mids of Aer, which was their intention. Instead, they got stuck in an in-between realm, the world of dreams and half-dreams. A perilous realm, where Cassían had been imprisoned by the Raven. It is a realm untouched by time completely. Lebía's willing death was the force needed to destroy the egg and push Ghavan back to the Lows of Aer."

That was the hardest part to accept. That, and the fact that the entire paradise in which Cassían had lived had been an elaborate prison concocted by the artisan, all to induce Cassían to forge a false covenant. And all of Vasyllia's problems historically had stemmed from that false covenant.

"So when I died, two things happened, yes?" Lebía tried to make sense of it. "One. My sacrifice made the twenty years of dream-scape the actual reality of Ghavan. But none of us have aged, except the children born in the egg reality. Is that... even possible?"

"Yes," said Alienne simply.

Mirnían laughed.

"The second thing," continued Lebía, "is that my sacrifice confirmed the true covenant, the covenant of Lassar the Blessed with the Unknown Father."

"Whom the Vasylli have always served," added Derzhava, "though after Cassían's mistake they confused the Unknown Father with Adonais. No fault of their own, but it was still enough for Vasyllia to fall to the Gumiren.

"Not the Gumiren," growled Batuk. "They are not true Gumiren. They are the Fallen." Etchigu nodded enthusiastically.

"And yet," Alienne said, "your sacrifice, Lebía, has changed the course of history. The way it had happened in history—you can read it in the apocryphal notes of Cassían, a copy of which is in Nebesta's Veche Library—Cassían *did* sacrifice Derzhava, who had been imprisoned with him by the artisan especially for that purpose. But when my husband Parfyon burned me before the gates of Vasyllia, he started a chain of events that shook the foundations of all the Realms. Time itself was fractured. I came into this Realm as Derzhava's protector. Then, you changed his sacrifice, and by doing so, placed self-sacrificial love at the foundation of the false covenant. It is as if you were the lump of metal out of which the covenant was forged. Not one covenant, you see now, but two. And no covenant with any evil Power can survive on a foundation of love. You have laid a crack at the foundation of the Raven's rule over Vasyllia. It is already beginning to end."

"So where do you come in, then?" asked Mirnían, looking at Batuk.

"We are the brothers of Khaidu," he said, but would say no more about who Khaidu was. "We were trapped in this Realm between the Realms as well. The lady Alienne offered us both a way out and a chance to avenge our losses at the hand of the Dark Father. We march with you to Vasyllia."

"Dark Father," murmured Alienne. "A fitting name for the Raven, indeed."

"But this Unknown Father," said Mirnían. "I don't understand. Who is he?"

"He is the one you have all worshipped in Adonais's name," said Derzhava, her eyes shining. Etchigu whispered to Batuk something in their tongue. She thought she heard the word, "seer." It was fitting. Derzhava was indeed a seer. "And he is the one whom Voran has gone to seek."

"The one for whose sake we must purify Vasyllia," said Alienne, "or rather, you must. I will send what help I can from the Lows. But I have died to the lower worlds."

Mirnían raised his tankard.

"Well, it is all a bit heady for me, but then, I have never been one for the mystical. It still keeps biting me on the heels though, and for once, I am glad of it. I raise my ale to you, allies of Vasyllia and foes of the Darkness. May the Unknown Father, his covenant forged out of the love of the Vasylli, raise us to be the Bane of the Raven."

The Gumiren stood up and started to sing something in their own tongue. It sent chills up Lebía's spine. Derzhava laughed with pure enjoyment.

"And so began the reclamation," she said, as though reciting a tale. Perhaps she was...

CHAPTER 12

TO BATTLE

Two weeks later, the long march of the combined armies of the Gumiren and Ghavanites reached the walls of Vasyllia. They lay in a heap of rubble and dead bodies. The land itself stank.

The seer Derzhava spoke in that day, before the gaping maw of the Raven's land.

"Here Alienne, the Golden Lady of the Lows of Aer, gave her life for love of her husband. Here, the foundations of all Realms cracked and moved, and time itself was rewritten. Here began the fall of the Raven, the rise of we who are his bane."

All the men hushed to listen to the words of the seer as she sat huddled in the arms of Lebía, who rode at the head of the column with her husband, the Dar of Vasyllia returned.

About a week later, they approached the Pass of Ardovían. Coming up to approach them was a beaten army, their banners as low as the shoulders of the warriors.

"Nebesti," said Mirnían to Lebía. "Perhaps Parfyon's men."

The warriors did not even try to raise their weapons. They merely trudged on toward the coming army of Ghavanites and Gumiren.

"Let them pass!" commanded Mirnían.

A litter approached, bearing a dead man. He was withered and white, and he looked as though the life had been sucked out of him. Lebía made the sign to avert evil. It came off him like the smell of something foul.

"That is the husband of Alienne the Golden Lady," said Derzhava the Seer, and all the warriors stopped to see the man who had fallen so low as to burn his own wife as an offering.

Over the pass they went, and before them in the valley an army was encamped. The banners were unfamiliar to Lebía, though Mirnían's eyes lit up as he saw them. The army seethed like an anthill disturbed by a dog.

"What is it, my love?" asked Lebía.

"I have heard of that banner. It is the banner of the Children of the Priest-King."

"Highness, look!" called one of the Ghavanite warriors.

Beyond that army, filling the narrow gap where the Vasyllia River passed toward the city, was yet another army. They bore the golden sun on black field.

"Traitors!" hissed Mirnían. "They've taken Father's banner for their own, the bastards."

"Call them what they are," said Batuk, who rode behind Mirnían. "They are the Fallen. Destined for the lowest pits of the land of the dead."

"Then let us send them the quicker to it, eh?" said Etchigu in his high tenor. He laughed, and with that ringing sound, the sun came out. No more than a silhouette, the figure of a red-clad warrior rode across the expanse of the sky. It brandished a spear that glinted off the sun, then it bowed at Mirnían.

"The Powers are with us this day, my friends," said Mirnían, unsheathing his sword. "Time to write new songs for new days. Forward!"

The combined armies of the Ghavanites and the Gumiren rode down the Pass of Ardovían.

Lebía watched them, her pride rising up with the tears from the depths of her heart.

Then, she gasped.

In her mind's eye, she saw her son, Antomír, lying dead by the side of a river, into which cherry blossoms fell like snow. *Again! What is the meaning of the vision?*

"Alienne sent it to you," said Derzhava from her litter. "The vision. *My* vision. While you were still asleep in Ghavan."

Lebía found she could say nothing through the tears that fell uncontrollably down her face.

"Be strong, my lady," Derzhava intoned. "You have changed history once. Perhaps you will change it once again."

Did you enjoy this book? You can make a big difference!

Reviews are the most powerful tools that I have when it comes to getting attention to my books. Although I'm not a starving artist, I don't have the financial muscle to take out full page ads in the *New York Times*.

But I do have something more powerful than that.

A committed, excited, and loyal group of readers.

If you've enjoyed my novel, I would be very grateful if you'd spend only five minutes to leave a short review on whatever book retailer you prefer.

Flip to the next page to read an excerpt from book 5 of the *Raven Son* series, *The Throne of the Gods*.

PRELUDE TO THE THRONE OF
THE GODS

PRELUDE

And behold, the Creator of the gods sat on his throne and spoke
the Realms into existence. His word became matter, his heart
became soul, and his spirit became spirit. And the songs of the
gods below him were beautiful and good, filling the chaos into forms
pleasing to eye and soul and spirit. Then the Creator of the Realms spoke.
A word so still, so small, that the Powers strained to hear it.

"Behold, I leave the throne vacant and go to my house. Whoever
wills to take my place on the throne, behold, it is vacant. But to the
violent who would take it, know this. The crown is heavy, and the seat is
onerous. Nevertheless, the Throne of the Gods suffers violence, and the
violent take it by force."

Apocryphal Book of the Raven
Author: Unknown

Fifteen years before the revelation of the Raven in the Heart of the
World...

Rogned, prince of Karila, balanced on the tip of the highest
point in his land. Before him plunged a sheer fall, thousands of
feet down to jagged, teeth-shaped rocks. Behind him a narrow

spur was all that kept him from another drop, down to a tarn said to be so deep that the bottom grazed the bones of the great serpent that formed the backbone of the world.

Something beyond the water pulled at him, calling with the intensity of a love song. He forced himself to look away.

Rogned had never quite appreciated the name of this crag—the Fang of the Giant—until this moment. It did not take a wild leap of the imagination to feel the stone heaving underneath him, as though an invisible upper jaw were coming down to meet the upward thrust of the Fang, to crush him before depositing him into a giant's gizzard.

The thought thrilled him: to be churned up and swallowed by the divine. It was what he had come here for, after all.

It had taken him most of the morning to climb the pock-marked Fang, through the bone-cutting winter wind and the ice-flecked mist. He thought he would never again hear anything other than the howl of the wind.

Better that than the screams of the dying in war, he thought.

From the top of the Fang he looked down at the green earth, and all sound ceased. The clouds tore apart slowly, silently. Three shafts of sunlight shot down into the land below him, and the tarn's frozen surface flashed.

Tears filled his eyes. He gritted his teeth until his jaw ached. Something like curdled milk filled him inside, something that would burst if he didn't let it out. He roared.

"How dare you reveal the land's beauty now?" he cried aloud to the Heights. "Now, when the grass and the rocks will be defiled with blood!"

No answer came from the Heights.

A flock of ravens flew underneath Rogned, bringing into sharp relief the army of five thousand Nebesti who were marching on Karila, his beloved home. Just three hundred fighting Karilans stood in the pass between the Fang and the Needle—an impossibly thin pillar of rock that reached half as high as the Fang. Kneeling, the Karilans faced the Needle—

sacred to their old gods, who had been suppressed by the victo-rious Vasyllian invaders, hundreds of years ago. But then Vasyllia fell, ending the confederacy of the three city-states of Vasyllia, Nebesta, and Karila. What followed was internecine slaughter, a war that was about to end with the total destruction of Karila, the runt of the three. How fitting that Nebesta, jealous first daughter of Vasyllia, would do the deed.

"Rogned!"

The voice was hardly more than a whisper in the howl of the wind. Rogned turned around, careful not to slip. The man who had followed him was past the first flower of youth, and his eyes were as deep as the tarn. Those eyes were filled with more pain, sorrow, and anguish than anything Rogned had ever seen. They called him the Healer. He healed everyone but himself.

"I was hoping you'd follow, Voran," said Rogned. "I wasn't sure you'd believed me."

"Have you finally lost your mind? I know you artisans are impulsive, but this?"

"It's halfway to the Heights," said Rogned, not trying to hide the elation that rose inside him. *Not long now.* Images from last night's dream flowed through his mind—a wing the color of lapis lazuli, an eye that blazed golden fire, the simultaneous pain and elation of the thrust of a giant sword through his heart.

A muffled roar rose up on a draft of warm wind. Rogned thought he could smell the stench of the sweat and fear of his people.

The Nebesti were no longer advancing in their perfect ranks. They were throwing themselves chaotically at the three hundred defenders of the city of Karila. Even from here, Rogned could smell their war lust.

"Quickly, Voran. This may be our only chance."

Voran's face blanched at the sight of the knife, which Rogned had pulled out of his boot in a smooth, practiced motion. He had rehearsed this moment many times during the last week.

"Rogned!" Voran's hands shook. The deep purple of the

shadows under his eyes made the paleness of his face ghostlike. "You're mad! Just because of a few dreams? You can't force an encounter with the Heights. High Beings come to you in their own time. You're just going to kill yourself."

"That's the idea," said Rogned. He sliced the knife across his left wrist. It hardly hurt at all, to his astonishment. It was even pleasant to feel the hot blood on his frozen skin.

"I promised myself no one else in your family would die!" Voran screamed as he ran to stop Rogned, nearly falling off the edge in his haste.

Too late.

A wave of exhaustion swept Rogned into unconsciousness. He fell, and there was no bottom. He kept falling and falling and . . . Rogned awoke in mid-fall.

What in all the . . .

He was no longer falling.

White sand as far as the eye could see. It crackled under him as he rose up from a crouching position. Now it felt more like glass than sand. Rogned's hands were covered in the stuff. Before he realized what he was doing, he licked his right thumb.

His eyes grew large in surprise.

Salt.

Then the immensity of the landscape pressed in on him from all sides, along with a smell like rotten eggs. There was nothing but salt—ranging from white to grey to slightly pink—in all directions. The sky above him looked like a mirror image of the salt. Perhaps the sky in this place was not blue.

Where am I?

A scented breeze played with his hair. His mind processed the smells—impossible in their profusion and intensity. There was orange there, and lilac, and morning grass after a spring downpour, and logs burning on the coldest evening of the year, and—

Rogned was running before his mind registered it. No, he wasn't running. There was no word for this. Each step was a leap miles long, as though his essence strove to tear itself out of his body and to dissipate in the perfection of that smell ahead of him.

His mind hiccupped—there was no other way to describe the way it was functioning as it tried to sift through the everything he saw, smelled, felt. But below thought, deeper, in the throbbing warmth of his chest, longing burned him.

I am going home. The thought rang out like a choir singing from a mountain peak.

Before his limping thoughts could retort—*what is home?*—something formed out of the shimmering mirages rising from the salt. A riot of color, spinning wildly, yet anchored more firmly than a mountain. A tower of white, whiter than any white he had ever seen. Walls encircling it. Seven of them, each made of stone that shimmered; and Rogned somehow knew it was harder than any stone he had ever seen in Karila. Set in the center of each encircling wall was a gate. They were too far away for him to make out the details, but they reminded him of what he thought diamonds must look like. He had only heard of diamonds in stories.

Trees, laden with red fruits with a golden innerglow, seemed to embrace him as he sped into their groves. They grew directly from the salt. Their smell—pomegranate mixed with cinnamon and honey—finally slowed him down. That and the winged giant with a sword made of lightning.

The giant's skin looked like marble—marble that was living tissue, not stone. His eyes shone bronze, and six wings of gold, lapis, emerald, ruby, silver, and topaz flickered in constant movement about his body. The lightning sword looked like a part of his arm, something as much belonging to him as the presence that emanated from him. The presence felt like a mountain about to fall on an ant.

Rogned fell on his knees, though the shaking of his hands was more joy than fear.

"You," Rogned whispered. His voice sounded foreign to this

place. He didn't belong here, and he was beginning to realize how mad he had been. And yet . . . how had he gotten here?

The giant spoke. "You came too early, child. My call was only a whisper. A preparation for a later time. No mortal can gain access to the Gardens of Aer before death."

"There will not be a later time," said Rogned, gathering courage from the shards of what was left of him after the voice of the giant had shattered him. "Karila is about to be wiped off the map. And I know my lessons: 'Those who take the Heights by force—they are the only ones worthy of it.'"

The giant laughed. Rogned had to look down at himself to make sure he had not burst into flame from its power.

"You quote scripture at me? I am of the Palymi, the highest order of the Powers that encircle the throne of the Unknown Father. We *inspired* that scripture."

"Then you know why I am here."

Something shifted in the Power's living-marble face, as though he were listening to a wind miles away.

"So you took the scriptures literally. You poor fool. You're not ready."

"I demand that the Heights answer the groan of Karila. We have been pushed back, inch by inch, forced to give up our lands, our very way of life to those who would exterminate us. I demand audience before the throne of the Unknown Father."

"You're lying."

If wind were a living thing with an emotion like anger, then it might have come close to what pressed Rogned to the salt-earth in that moment.

"You do not come here with a desire for justice. Do you not realize that I can see through you?"

Images and emotions bubbled up, pressing on his brain. His elder brother Karakul's dead body on top of a pyre. The fury Rogned had felt at seeing it. The urge for vengeance that boiled inside. The desire to tear down Vasyllia for what it had done to his brother. The burning madness of artistic creation.

The sense of being possessed by an outside force when he sculpted. The feeling of power over the whole earth, as though he could turn it inside out at his own whim. The thought that he so often pushed down, though he gave himself over to it in his dreams—*I am touched by the divine. Only I can stop the war.*

Rogned grabbed his head, trying to ward off the onslaught of his own thoughts. His heart beat savagely, as if it were going to burst.

"Pride, anger, vengeance. Smallness of mind. Of such are the Gardens of Aer?" The giant seemed to grow even higher. "Raw metal in my hands. That's what you are. Don't you understand? Until you've been tempered, the fire of my power will melt you, not make you stronger."

"And what of courage?" Rogned pushed himself up to his feet, grinding his teeth against the power pushing him down. "What man has courage like mine? I'm not doing it for myself! I do it for little Nadina, the five-year-old who lost both her parents in a raid by the Nebesti last week. For my brother, who was murdered by a man he loved like a father. For all those innocents who are being destroyed, wiped off this good earth, punished for crimes and sins they didn't commit."

The sword flashed upward. Rogned's anger blazed out of him so hot, he thought he would be immolated in it.

"No! I know you, Palymi," Rogned said. "You guide my hand when I sculpt. That work of putting chaos into a form more perfect than creation itself—you and I have done that together. Don't deny it! I *know* you. You will give this to me, because it is the only way left. The war will tear the land apart. There will be no one left to worship at any altar."

The sword plunged into his heart. Rogned screamed.

Through the firelight of that agony, he saw the giant step aside. The first gate to the Gardens of Aer stood open before him. Flowers and trees of color and variety that he could never have imagined—they beckoned to him. No human love impelled

like this. Rogned rose up, through the agony, and ran to the door
. . .

The world yanked up from underneath him, and wet mist
covered his face.

❦

"There!" Voran gasped, hovering over Rogned. The shadows
under his eyes were even darker than before. "I made a promise
to you, Rogned, when you were a boy. Did you forget? I will not
let you die in vain. Not after your brother died. I loved him, you
know. He was the brother I never had . . ."

Rogned couldn't understand what Voran was saying. All he
heard in his head was the song of the paradise birds nesting in
the Gardens of Aer; all he could smell was the tuberose and
lavender and . . .

A foul wind inundated him with the coppery smell of blood.
Rogned gagged, his hands flailing. He grabbed Voran's head and
squeezed it. Every muscle in his body strained. He screamed.

"Rogned, I brought you back. You won't die now." Voran
wheezed, trying to pull apart Rogned's hands. He was too weak.

"What have you done?" screamed Rogned. It echoed, the
sound bouncing around them as though they were in a cavern. "I
was so . . . so close!"

He threw Voran aside, not even caring anymore if he fell off
the edge of the Fang. The clouds above him churned with wind,
pregnant with sleet. He reached for them. He could feel them
between his hands like clay, like stone melting in his hands,
forming into a shape. He gasped. Pleasure filled him, a rip
current to the wave of disgust that now fell off him like rainwa-
ter. He . . . *sculpted the clouds.*

After the waves of pleasure had risen so high that his breath
caught in his throat, he finally exhaled. The sun broke through
the sculpture of fog and mist and ice and snow that he had made
and that covered the expanse of the entire sky. It was the most

beautiful thing he had ever done. The most beautiful thing any human being had ever done. He felt the Palymi's sword in his chest again.

"Yes," he said aloud, as his mind unmoored from his body. The word sounded distant, as though someone else were saying it. "I know now. Beauty *will* save this world."

☸

Three days later, Rogned woke up. He lay inside a battle tent on the most comfortable pallet he had ever felt. He was so confused, he hadn't even remembered his own name at first. Voran had explained everything to him—how the sculpture he had created had stopped all the warriors in their tracks. How all of them had put their arms down, some of them openly weeping at the sight, some in such fear that they ran away screaming. The leaders of both sides had immediately come together to discuss terms of peace.

"Everyone agreed," said Voran. "You, Rogned, could be the only one to lead a new, unified army of the Three Cities. You've ended the internecine war. They're calling you the prophet-prince already."

☸

Food no longer tasted like food. Even the salt in the barren wasteland bordering the Gardens of Aer had teased his sense of taste with hints of pomegranate and mint. Food was like sand now. Drink couldn't fill Rogned—it only left a gaping abyss inside that seemed to grow with every goblet. People's conversation grated like cracked cymbals. Voran's company, which he had treasured only weeks before, preferring it to the company of anyone else, cut at him like knife thrusts. The only comfort he had was in walking, alone, among the sharp rocks.

There was whispering life in those rocks, a sliver of that same power that pulsed through the lands bordering the Gardens of Aer. He would stand before the Fang, his hands pressed to the cold stone, and the twisting agony in his chest, like thorns slowly burrowing into flesh, would fade to a dull ache.

One evening, he was walking back to the now unified camp of the two armies. They would soon begin the long journey to a place Voran called Ghavan Isle, to be presented as the new army of the Three Cities to Dar-in-Exile Mirnían of Vasyllia. It had been Voran's idea, of course. But Rogned supported it. As much as he could muster support for anything these days.

The hundreds of campfires looked like clouds of fireflies. And they felt just as ephemeral. The two armies couldn't possibly remain this friendly for long. Rogned wanted nothing to do with the coming war for Vasyllia's reclamation. Not yet, at least. He wanted his final, fading memories of the Palymi's presence.

He drifted through the knots of waiting warriors—eating, drinking, laughing, telling stories, simply staring into the night. He avoided them, as though he were an incarnate wind. As he passed by them, he heard snatches of conversation.

". . . like a tower . . . just like old Nebesta, but greater by far . . ."

". . . a watchtower on top, the fires reaching up higher than anything . . . a beacon to the Heights . . ."

They were talking about his sculpture, he realized. But something was wrong. These men were Nebesti, but in the adjoining Karila camp, two old men were mumbling to each other in archaic Karilan:

". . . the rusted blade reforged, held in the hand of a Karakul reborn . . ."

"Yes, I recognized his face. Of course Rogned would put his own brother on the greatest work of art any man had ever made . . ."

They were talking about the same sculpture. But . . .

With a sinking feeling, Rogned realized he had no memory of

the sculpting. Not the process, not the form, not even what it looked like.

He rushed back to his tent. The firelight threw back two shadows inside. Rogned heard Voran talking to the chief of Nebesta's armies, a hard man named Yarpolk Dolgoruk.

"Are you mad? We all saw it! It was Vasyllia restored, every stone of it more glorious than it had ever been in years past!"

Yarpolk sniggered. "You *would* see that, you fanatic. Can't you get it through your thick skull? Vasyllia is fallen. And if we ever come near it again, I would prefer to take each stone apart and pulverize it, not to put it all back together again!"

"What did you see, then?" challenged Voran, but Rogned heard a note of doubt in his voice.

"The River Nebestaala, a perfect sun rising over it. Two spears of fire and light crossed above it."

"That's . . . wait . . . that's . . ."

Rogned fled. He thought he knew what had happened. His heart plunged to his feet.

Every person saw what he needed most in the sculpture.

There would be no peace. There would be no end to war. As soon as everyone realized what had happened, the old tribalism would cause fissures in the new unity. There could be no unity behind a prophet-prince who gave a different prophecy for each of his followers.

What madness! He could never lead. What was he thinking?

It struck him like a punch in the face—intense, shrieking longing. The Garden. It called to him.

What are you doing, playing power games? You can only help them in one way. Voran stopped you the first time. Now is the time to finish the journey.

Was it his own thought? Rogned didn't care anymore.

Rogned stood on the Fang in the light of the full moon. The tarn below him sparkled in the moonlight. There was music in the air, faint, barely audible, like a lone violin droning a single, plangent note. He recognized it. It was coming from the other side of the water. All he needed to do was jump.

He jumped.

The Throne of the Gods **is available for sale on all retailers in ebook and paperback format. Audiobook format is coming later in 2021.**

ALSO BY NICHOLAS KOTAR

The Raven Son Series:
The Song of the Sirin
The Curse of the Raven
The Heart of the World
The Forge of the Covenant
The Throne of the Gods

The Worldbuilding Series:
How to Survive a Russian Fairy Tale
Heroes for All Time
A Window to the Russian Soul

Russian Fairy Tales and Myths:
In a Certain Kingdom: Fairy Tales of Old Russia

ABOUT THE AUTHOR

Nicholas Kotar is a writer of epic fantasy inspired by Russian fairy tales, a freelance translator from Russian to English, the resident conductor of the men's choir at a Russian monastery in the middle of nowhere, and a semi-professional vocalist. His one great regret in life is that he was not born in the nineteenth century in St. Petersburg, but he is doing everything he can to remedy that error.

Made in the USA
Monee, IL
31 May 2024

59185381R00069